Thomas

His Defenders

Book 2

By

Ronna M. Bacon

Deuteronomy 31:6 Be strong and courageous. Do not fear or be in dread of them, for it is the Lord your God who goes with you. He will not leave you or forsake you.

NKJV

Table of Contents

Chapter 1
Chapter 2
Chapter 3
Chapter 4
Chapter 5
Chapter 6
Chapter 7
Chapter 8
Chapter 9
Chapter 10
Chapter 11
Chapter 12
Chapter 13
Chapter 14
Chapter 15
Chapter 16
Chapter 17
Chapter 18
Chapter 19
Chapter 20
Chapter 21
Chapter 22
Chapter 23
Chapter 24
Chapter 25
Chapter 26
Chapter 27
Chapter 28
Chapter 29
Chapter 30
Chapter 31

Chapter 32
Chapter 33
Chapter 34
Chapter 35
Chapter 36
Chapter 37
Chapter 38
Chapter 39
Chapter 40
Chapter 41
Epilogue
Dear Readers

Chapter 1

Dashing across the parking lot near a downtown building, Thomas Brant dodged the puddles that had accumulated after the heavy rain overnight. It was late spring but the day was damp and cold. He tugged the green ball cap down over his golden blond hair that brushed the turned-up collar of his jean jacket. His amber eyes were on the move, searching the area around him. It had become a habit with him as a member of a security team located in Oak City to be on guard always. Thomas felt something off but couldn't pinpoint exactly what it was.

Pulling open the door, he smiled at the older lady who had appeared in front of him, hesitating before she exited. A quiet thank you reached to his ears. He nodded at her and then entered. He didn't normally shop at pharmacies but today he had offered to pick up a prescription for an older friend and neighbour who was housebound.

Walking quickly through the store, Thomas' smile turned to a frown. He paused before he approached the prescription pick-up window, his frown deepening. There was something definitely off that morning; his senses told him that. He just didn't know what it was.

The prescription tucked away in his truck, Thomas turned, feeling someone approaching him. He spun, unable to duck the fist heading for his face. Off balance, Thomas felt his arms wrestled behind him and then handcuffs clicking on his wrists. He struggled to

—

escape but was unable to do so before he was forced away from his truck and towards another vehicle.

Thomas could faintly hear the scream of a lady and then silence. Landing hard on the truck seat, he struggled to sit upright but a hand shoved at his back, holding him down. He sensed that someone else had landed on the seat beside him and could hear angry words without understanding them. It was a lady's voice, that much he knew.

The truck took off at high speed, leaving the onlookers standing stunned at the abduction that they had just witnessed. One brave soul ran for his own vehicle, trying to follow the truck but losing it as it made many fast turns. He returned to the pharmacy, finding the parking lot full of patrol vehicles, the red and blue lights flashing in a wild manner.

Pulled abruptly from the vehicle, Thomas stumbled as he was shoved forcibly forward toward a building. He had trouble with his balance, his hands still cuffed behind him. His head was aching from the savage blow that he had taken. Shoved forward once more, he stumbled again and was just unable to remain on his feet. He hit his knees and then fell forward, to land awkwardly. The breath was driven from him.

Once more, Thomas could hear the sounds of a lady's voice, demanding that they be released and that the handcuffs be removed. He heard the loud slap that sounded and then her whimpers of pain. His eyes blurring as he looked around, he could vaguely see the huddled form near him. He felt the handcuffs removed from his wrists but was too stunned to react. His vision faded as he lost consciousness. The kick to his ribs that he had just received had taken his breath before he was lost to his surroundings.

Taran Byrne remained huddled in a heap, a hand cupping her face to try and ease the intense pain that she was feeling. Tears trickled down her cheeks, tears that she would never have shed if things had been different. She blinked, trying to focus on her surroundings and then on the man with her. She didn't think that she knew him, but that fact was something Taran was not sure about.

A few hours later, Taran sat up, her hand on her face. She could feel the swelling and felt her lip. The cut stung as her tongue touched it. Taran was suddenly, deeply afraid. She had only been walking towards the pharmacy where she worked as a pharmacist when she saw the assault on the man. Her scream had attracted the attackers' attention and somehow she found herself grabbed and shoved into the truck as well.

On her feet, Taran approached the man, a toe out to nudge him. He didn't move. Dropping to her knees, her hands rolled him to his back, one of his arms flopping lifelessly across his chest. Reaching for a wrist, Taran was glad to feel a pulse. That didn't make it any easier, though, to be alone with him.

Once more rising, she walked the room, looking for a way out. Turning the doorknob and tugging at it showed that the door was indeed locked. The windows too were barricaded in some way. Taran could not just decide how.

A groan had her turning in fear, a hand covering her mouth to stifle her scream. Taran stared at Thomas, seeing his head was beginning to toss. Back on her knees beside her, her hand rested on his cheek, stopping his movement for a moment before the motions became more rapid.

"Sir? Please wake up! I need you to wake up!" Taran winced as her voice sounded too loud in the room. She shook Thomas gently, not able to rouse him. She felt at his face, seeing the bruising that was starting. On her feet once more, she headed for the ensuite that she had found earlier. A cloth was rinsed out in as cold of water as she could before she was back on her knees beside him. Taran placed the folded cloth on the redness and bruising, hearing a soft sigh come from him.

Taran sat back on her heels, studying Thomas closer. She gave a sigh herself as she recognized him from church. She knew his name and that he worked for a security team. She just didn't know him.

Thomas stirred a few hours later, feeling his head raised to allow him to swallow water. His eyes opened and he gazed around, stopping as they found Taran.

"What happened?" Thomas had to clear his throat in order to speak. "Where are we? And who are you?"

"You were knocked out. We were kidnapped. And I'm Taran. I know you from seeing you at church." Tarn sat beside Thomas, a hand resting on his shoulder. "You shouldn't be moving. You've been unconscious for hours."

"I have? What time is it?" Thomas struggled to sit up, Taran linking an arm with him to help him stay upright. He fought the nausea that hit him as his body raised. He certainly didn't want to embarrass himself by being sick in front of a lady.

"It's about four in the afternoon. We were kidnapped just after nine. I was heading in to start work at 9:30. I never made it. And my family and friends will be so worried." Taran had trouble controlling her emotions.

Thomas gave a growl of distress and then just wrapped her into a hug. Taran was startled at first and then hugged him back. She usually avoided any contact with a man other than those in her family but this was different. They were together in danger. She sensed that he would protect her, even to putting his own life at risk.

Hearing the lock open, Thomas peered that way. He was still having difficulty seeing. He sighed to himself at that. He had a concussion, he had no doubt of that, and needed help. Thomas just didn't think that he would receive that any time soon.

One of their abductors stood there, a tray in his hands. He set it on the floor and then backed out of the room, the door locked behind him. They could not get a description of him as he had been wearing a surgical mask and sunglasses.

Taran stared at the tray of food before she was on her feet to retrieve it. She set it down beside Thomas, not sure if they should be eating it or not.

"Do we eat it, Thomas?" Taran's voice was subdued.

"I have no idea, Taran, is it?" Thomas reached for a packaged sandwich and felt the plastic. "I don't see that it has been tampered with. We need to eat, Taran. And do you have any idea where we are?"

Taran shrugged, her eyes on her hands. She had a vague idea where they were but she wasn't sure why.

"We were taken to the outskirts of town, Thomas. It's a really nice house. I don't know the address or owner though." Taran shifted her seating, curling her legs up beside her. "Have you any idea why?"

Thomas shook his head. He took in the long dark brown hair that fell in waves below her shoulders and the deep green of her eyes, shadowed now with fear.

"I don't. All I was doing was picking up a prescription for a neighbour who couldn't get out." Thomas drew in a deep breath. "God is here, Taran. I have no doubt about that. He is protecting up and will defend us. Now, we need to pray. That's the only way that we'll ever get out of this." Thomas simply reached for her hand, finding her not resisting his tight grasp on hers. His head bowed as he began to petition God to release them and heal them.

Chapter 2

Thomas staggered to his feet, swaying as he stood. Taran's arms were around him to help steady him. His own arm rested around her as his eyes closed for a moment. Opening his eyes again, he searched the room through blurry eyes. Taran turned him towards the bathroom, walking away after the door closed.

Starting at himself in the mirror above the sink, Thomas shook his head and instantly regretted it. The headache pounded fiercely for a moment before it eased to some extent. His hand felt at his jaw, finding the lump and the bruising. He winced as he touched it.

A cold cloth held to his face, Thomas opened the door once more, searching for the lady. He frowned as he saw her. He knew her from seeing her at church and around town. He knew that she said that her name was Taran.

Taran spun from where she stood at a window, staring out into the night. She was beside him again, an arm around him to help him walk towards the centre of the room. It was a nice room, she decided, but would be even nicer with furniture. Blankets were piled in the corner. She had shaken out some to make pallets for Thomas and herself. Her hands were gentle as she helped him to sit on one of them.

"How are you feeling?" Her voice was low, almost too low for Thomas to hear.

He shrugged, not sure how to respond. Thomas knew that he was hurt and held captive.

"We need to get away." His voice was raspy for a moment.

"There's no way out. The door is locked. The windows are sealed shut." Taran didn't think that they would be able to escape, ever. They would be captive for years.

"We'll find a way, Taran. Right now, I need to sleep." Thomas' body could not hold him upright any more.

Taran brushed at the hair on his forehead before she tucked the cold cloth against his face. She was on her feet, reaching for another blanket to cover him. Sitting near him on her own pallet, Taran began to pray as she never had in her life. She knew that God was there and that He was in control. It was just so hard to trust Him in this.

Neither of them heard the door unlock and open. The employer of the men who had them kidnapped stood over them, a dark look on his face. He was angry that Thomas had been hurt. He needed him well and on his feet. He had plans for him.

His gaze turned to Taran. She was not to be here. She was incidental to what happened. He frowned before he nodded. He decided that he would use her as well in his plans, plans that would ruin the two of them and destroy their families. That was incidental to his plans.

Taran stirred slightly, her eyes opening for a moment before she slept again. The snicking of the closing lock had roused her. She shifted how she was lying to study Thomas. Her eyes closed and she slept again.

Early in the morning, Thomas roused, his senses telling him that he was not alone. He waited for someone to move or speak. When that didn't happen, he cracked his eyes open and stared around. His gaze stopped on Taran before he frowned. Thomas raised himself upright, waiting for his head to clear before he stood. He stared down at Taran, a puzzled look on his face.

Sighing, Thomas walked the room, trying the door to find it locked. He tried to raise the windows but was stymied in his attempts to raise them. He stared out, noting that they were on the first floor and that there wasn't much of a drop to the ground. Thomas jumped as he felt a hand on his back.

Taran stood there, a frown on her face that cleared as she saw that Thomas' eyes were clearer.

"Thomas? It's really early. What are your thoughts?" Taran's voice was low.

"That we need to get out of here. It's really early." He squinted at his watch in the low light that was on in the room. "It's four in the morning." He studied her. "Are you ready to run?"

"Whenever you are. How, though?" Taran was puzzled as to how they could escape.

"The window. I think that I can break it quietly enough so that no one hears us." Thomas leaned on a pane of glass, hearing it crack. He carefully worked away to remove the small pains of glass and then the

—

wood that had been holding the panes. He looked around as Taran gave a sound. "Is someone there?"

Taran had moved to the door, an ear placed against it. She shook her head before she almost ran across the room towards him.

"Let me go first and then I'll help you." Thomas was as good as his word, escaping through the window and then reaching up to grasp her around the waist as she clambered through the opening after him.

Thomas flattened them against the house, searching for any sign of someone who had heard the slight noises that he had made. Seeing no one, he reached for Taran's hand, finding hers reaching for his. He tugged her after him as he ran through the backyard. Stymied for a moment by the fence, he jumped and caught at the top of it. Hanging on with one hand, his other hand reached to help Taran as she too jumped for the fence, reaching for the top.

They scrambled over the fence and then dropped to the ground. Thomas' eyes closed momentarily at the pain in his head that the jar of landing on the ground caused. He felt Taran's hand on his face before he just reached to hug her. With her hand in his once more, they took off on a run, heading away from the house and towards town. Thomas had a fair idea of where they were and whose house it was, but he wasn't totally sure about the owner. He would need to find Aidan McNeill, a police detective friend, and let him know where they had been secreted. And secreted they had been. Thomas had no doubt that harm had been meant towards him.

———

Taran tugged at his hand at last, stopping and gasping for air. She was a runner but never running for her life. She bent over, her hands on her knees, trying to regain her breath. Thomas stood beside her, breathing hard, a hand resting on her back. His eyes were in constant motion, searching for their abductors or anyone else that meant them harm.

He reached for Taran's hand again, tugging her into a fast walk. Thomas knew that it would not be long before they were discovered missing and then the search for them would be on. His steps hesitated as he neared the downtown area and a man appeared in front of him. Thomas' eyes narrowed as he studied him before he nodded, walking after him, Taran keeping pace with him.

Chapter 3

Oak City Police Detective Aidan McNeill paused as he stared at Thomas' truck the day that Thomas and Taran disappeared. He had been on the scene of another crime nearby when the call about the abduction had come in. He had paused in his steps towards his car as he heard the names come across the air waves.

The patrol officer walked towards him, a hand raised to stop Aidan.

"Jimmy? What do we have?" Aidan had to admit to himself that he was worried about Thomas.

"Thomas. He's disappeared. From what we can gather, he picked up a prescription for his neighbour. I can see it on the front seat of his truck. He disappeared right after that. The thing of it is, Taran Byrne disappeared at the same time." Jimmy looked back towards the pharmacy. "She was due to work today, starting at 9:30. We have evidence that Thomas left the pharmacy about 9:20."

"And it's what? 9:45 now?" Aidan paced around the techs working the scene. "Any eyewitnesses?"

"We do have them. They stated that Thomas and Taran were forced into a truck. Thomas was hurt by what they said. How seriously, they just didn't know. Taran didn't seem to be hurt."

"Tell me that we have a description and plate number." Aidan was praying that was the case. He didn't want another friend going through what Thomas' team member, Paul, had gone through with his lady, Payten.

"We have a description. We're working on a plate number from the surveillance cameras around here. I'm not hopeful that we can get that. The consensus seemed to be that it had no plate or the plate was covered up." Jimmy pointed to a man standing nearby. "He's the one who gave the best description of what happened."

Aidan nodded, just standing and staring at the scene. His thoughts were muddled for a moment, but he was definitely praying for his friend. Taran he knew from church, being part of the same Bible study group.

He walked at last towards the man, his head tilting.

"Jacob Riley? What can you tell me?" Aidan paused in front of him, his notebook and pen out.

"Not much more than I told Jimmy, Aidan. I was parking when I saw the commotion. Thomas took a blow to the face. I couldn't tell if it knocked him out or not. Taran was walking across the parking lot and they nabbed her as well. I don't know that she was meant to go with them. She put up a good fight. As to the truck? It was a diesel truck, full cab, with dual wheels on the back. White in colour. I couldn't see the plate. I have a feeling that it wasn't there or covered enough that you couldn't see it."

"Thanks, Jacob. We'll likely have more questions for you about that. The men?" Aidan was hoping that he had more description of them.

———

"Not a lot to tell you about them. They were disguised. Surgical masks. Sunglasses. Ball caps. Hoodies with the hoods pulled up. They worked together as a team. I would suspect that they have done this before. They were in and out in just a couple of moments, not longer enough for anyone of us to call for help or prevent it."

"Thanks, Jacob. This helps." Aidan walked away, heading for the pharmacy and the staff there.

Thirty minutes later, he stopped near Thomas' truck. They needed to move it. The techs had not found any evidence on it. It did concern Aidan that the neighbour's prescription was still there. He turned as he heard his name called and walked towards the man waiting.

"Titus? You're here?" Aidan reached to shake Thomas' brother's hand.

"I am. They called me about Thomas, something about him being missing?" Titus was worried about his brother.

"Thomas is missing. He was taken from here. We don't have a lot of information on that. The thing is that Taran Byrne went missing with him."

"Taran? I know of her from around church. She's a pharmacist here." Titus nodded towards the store. "In there, if I'm correct."

"That's correct. Listen? You don't happen to have a spare key to his truck, do you?" Aidan didn't think that he would.

"Actually, I do. Dad's waiting over there for me." Titus pointed behind him. "I can take Thomas' truck to his home. But I don't understand why."

"None of us do at this point. I'll need to speak with you and your parents. It's all part of the investigation."

"Taran? What about her people? I don't know if I have ever heard her speak of them."

"I have reached out to her parents. Unfortunately, they are traveling overseas and can't be reached readily. I will continue to reach out to them." Aidan looked around. "It looks as if it's clear for you to take your brother's truck. I'll follow you."

Titus sat in Thomas' driveway for a moment before he was out of the truck and running for the door. Unlocking it, he quickly fingered in his security code and then walked rapidly through the house. He could hear his father's voice and Aidan's as they did the same.

"He's not here, Dad." Titus walked towards his father. "I was praying that he was."

"So was I, son. I did speak with Gideon. He'll get the prayer chain working." Thaddeus spoke about their pastor. "He'll be around the house later, he said."

"Thanks, Dad. Aidan? What else can we do?"

"At the moment? I'm not really sure. For now, I'll start with his team and then work out from them." Aidan had reached out to Don, the security team leader who Thomas worked for. "He'll start working with the other four to see what they can come up with. I need a list of his friends and enemies if you know of any of the latter. Now, head off. Lock up. A patrol vehicle will be around overnight. And I will be in contact with you."

Aidan watched them walk away, hearing footsteps walking towards him. He sighed before he turned. Don and the other four on the team, Paul, Mark, Joshua, and Caleb, stood in front of him.

"Aidan? What can we do?" Don spoke for the group.

"As of now? We need a list of anyone who has threatened Thomas that you are aware of. And then we start working it. And yes, I have spoken with Toryn. He's aware of what's happened." Toryn was the Oak City police chief but also a close friend of Don's team.

Chapter 4

Aidan walked around Thomas' house the next day, not seeing any evidence that he had been there. He had also done the same at Taran's. He was worried about his friend. This was not what any one of them wanted. There had been no real evidence found the day before. And the descriptions of the men didn't help. He turned as he felt someone near him.

Don stood there, his eyes on Thomas' house. He had spent the night in prayer for his friend. This was the second one of his team to go through danger like this. Paul and his lady, Payten, had survived and were planning their wedding in the near future. Don had prayed that the rest of them escaped whatever it was, but it seemed that Thomas had not.

"Aidan? Any word?" Don's voice sounded loud in the silence near the house. He could hear the sound of lawn mowers in the distance and the barking of dogs and shouts of young children. Thomas lived in a family-friendly neighbourhood and was a welcome part of that community, willing to help anyone who had a need.

"No. Not one. I spoke with his parents and brother. They haven't received any ransom demand. I've walked the perimeter of the yard and around the house. There is nothing here." Aidan was frustrated. There should be word of some kind but there wasn't.

"I didn't think that there would be. My team is meeting this morning to go over any case that we feel may have bearing on this. The thing is that my guys

—

are well liked. Even when we have difficulty with a client, we walk away from it, pray about it, and set it aside. We have never had a sense that anyone was after any of us. That was, until Paul went through what he did.”

“That’s a puzzle for sure, Don. And there was something that always seemed left over from that. We never did explain the bombs.” Aidan walked back towards his car, turning to lean against his. He watched Don, seeing the stress that he was trying hard to hide.

“We didn’t. We’ve prayed for my team, hoping against hope that none of the rest of us underwent anything.” Don leaned against the car as well, watching as the elderly neighbour next door stood on her porch. He frowned before he walked her way. “Mrs. Wright? Are you okay?”

“No, I don’t know that I am.” The light breeze stirred her white curls. “Is Thomas home yet?”

“No, he’s not. You did get your medication last night?” Don stood beside her, his head tilted to watch her closely.

“I did, thank you, Don. Titus brought it over. He said that Thomas wasn’t able to do that but didn’t explain. I haven’t seen him today. Is he okay?” Thomas was a favourite of hers, spending time listening to her tales of being a teacher.

“No, he’s not. He’s missing.” Don’s hand gently caught her arm as she swayed before he turned her to sit on one of the chairs on her porch. He heard Aidan’s steps behind him. “Are you okay?”

———

"I don't know that I am." She frowned at him, her eyes still keen despite being retired and elderly. "Maybe that explains the truck that I saw two days ago cruising the neighbourhood as we said in our youth."

"A truck?" Aidan crouched down near her. "Mrs. Wright? Can you tell me about it?"

"I can do better. I printed off a picture from my security system. I was going to call your office, Aidan, but didn't get a chance to. Go on in, Titus. It's on the kitchen counter. Bring it out for Aidan." She shooed him away with a wave of her hand, leaving Aidan grinning at her. She was a favourite of the men, having taught them English in high school. "Now, I couldn't tell how many men were in it. I know of two on the front seat but I couldn't tell about the back because of the window tint. I wish that I had called it in. Maybe Thomas wouldn't be missing."

"Mrs. Wright? I need to ask you a question. Do you know Taran Byrne?" Aidan finally rose to sit in a chair nearby, knowing that Titus had done the same.

"Taran? Why?" Her face paled for a moment before determination took over. "She's missing? I wondered. I heard the news report simply stating that your department was investigating what was thought to be an abduction of two people."

"She is, Mrs. Wright. What can you tell me about her?" Aidan's notepad was out as he posed his pen over it.

"Taran? She's a very smart lady. She graduated high school at age 16 and then went off to college. She graduated as a pharmacist at age 19. She was young

—

but the owner of the pharmacy didn't hold it against her. She's been there for ten years and is well loved by everyone there. She stops by once in a while, just to share a meal with me." Mrs. Wright blinked for a moment, her eyes on Titus. "Find them, boys. Don't let any harm come to them. As to their friends, their families can likely tell you better than I can, Aidan." She was on her feet, moving towards her front door, closing it after her.

The two men had risen to their feet when she had stood, watching her closely before they shared a look. Titus shrugged and then walked way, heading for Thomas' house. He unlocked the door, reaching for the mail in the box before he did so. He set the mail tidily on his brother's desk before he sat in the black leather chair behind it. Titus' head dropped as he began to pray for his brother. He wanted him home and now.

Aidan walked away, not having known that about Taran. No one had thought to tell him. He reached for his phone which had kept vibrating. He frowned at the text before he was running for his vehicle and taking off with the lights and sirens on. He was needed on another scene. There were just too many investigations.

Thaddeus and Rose hesitated at the door to their son's home. It was open and they prayed it was because Thomas was at home. They sighed in disappointment as Titus appeared.

"Titus? Any word this morning?" Rose reached to hug her son, wondering at how tall he was.

"No, there isn't, Mom. Aidan was here when I got here. He doesn't have any word on Thomas or Taran." Titus struggled to control his emotions. He depended on his brother who was just one year old than him. They were close brothers. It hurt that Thomas was missing.

Thaddeus hugged his son, holding on just a little bit longer than normal. He was hurting for his sons, both of them. He just didn't know how to comfort Titus or even Rose. All he could do was petition God to protect his oldest son.

Chapter 5

Pausing his footsteps once more, Thomas gripped Taran's hand tighter in his. He searched for a safe place to hide until he could reach out for help. His hand felt his jacket pocket before he frowned.

"Taran? Do you have your phone?" Thomas kept his voice low.

"No. I had forgotten it at home yesterday. I didn't think too much about it, knowing that I could use the pharmacy phone if I needed to. Anyone who wanted to reach me would just leave a voice mail or send a text message." She looked around. "How safe are we?"

"As safe as we can be for now." Thomas headed towards a building that was rundown. "In here, for now, I think, Taran. I need to call in help." He tugged at her hand, not sure why she wasn't moving with him. "Taran?"

"Thomas? I don't think that we can do that." There was fear in her voice.

"Why not?" Thomas turned, his eyes closing for a moment. No, they would not be safe, not with the men standing around them. "Didn't we just do this?"

"We did, Mr. Brant. This time, you're coming with us. This time? You're not getting away. We still don't understand how you were able to break the window without alerting us." The man pointed a weapon at Taran. "Now, move. We're heading away from here and to our truck. This time, we'll lock you up where you can't escape." The man's anger lashed at the couple.

Thomas' hesitated before he felt the weapon nudge him hard in the back. He walked forward slowly, desperate to find a way out. Only there didn't seem to be one. Thomas frowned as he heard a slight sound to his left. He refused to look that way, knowing if he did that someone might well be hurt.

Taran shot a quick glance past Thomas, a frown covering her face as she caught glimpse of someone watching them and then ducking behind cover. Was it someone who could help them? *Lord, please protect us. I know that You are here. I know that You hear our prayers. Please, Lord, we need to get away. I don't know that we'll survive if we don't. I don't understand the why or who. You are in control of this. Please, Lord, at least let Thomas escape. I don't care about myself. Thank you, Lord, for hearing my petition.*

Thomas paused at a red light, sensing that the men had put away their weapons, yet still stood near them. He glanced at the traffic and then down at Taran. If they crossed that street, then they would disappear once more. And this time, he didn't think that they would reappear for a long time, if ever. His instincts and training had kicked in. Thomas was assessing the situation, trying desperately to find a way out. He frowned at the men watching him from across the street, seeing a faint nod from one. He drew in a deep breath. This is where it would get dangerous, he knew. The group across the street was waiting for them and would move in to try and separate Thomas and Taran from their abductors. They were willing to put themselves at risk to accomplish that.

Taran frowned as she too stared across the street. She recognized some of the men from her work with the homeless shelter. She sighed. *They're ready to put themselves out there, aren't they? Protect them, Lord. Don't let anyone be hurt because of me. I don't know that I can live with that if they are.*

Thomas tightened his grip on Taran as the light turned green. A poke from a finger forced him forward. He watched the group approaching them. They made no effort to move out of their way, simply surrounding the five and then moving inbetween Thomas and Taran and their abductors. The group turned as a unit and moved back the way that they had just come, Thomas and Taran in the very centre of the group.

Hearing the yells of frustration and anger from the men, Thomas picked up his pace, feeling the crowd pushing them forward at a more rapid pace. They were shoved into a building, through it, and then through three more. Taran could feel herself drawing on the reserves in her body that she never knew that she had, just in an attempt to stay with Thomas and the crowd or mob or whatever it was called. Without his grasp on her hand, she was sure that she would have fallen.

Shoving the couple into another building, the mob dispersed, leaving Thomas staring at the door and then at Taran. He simply reached to wrap her into a hug, his chest heaving from the rapid pace at which they had been moved.

—

"Taran? You're okay?" Thomas kept his voice low, his head bent so that he could whisper in her ear.

"I am. What just happened?" Taran leaned back to look up at him, taking in the stress and pain on his handsome face. "You're hurting, Thomas."

"I am. We need to find somewhere to hide. This building? We were brought here for a reason." Thomas walked away from her, searching for the hidden room that he had been told about. He found it and then beckoned her forward, shoving her inside and closing the wall after him. "Here, sit on this pallet. You need to rest."

Taran's hand reached for his, pulling him down beside her.

"You do too. Your head is hurting you more than you want to admit."

"It is." Thomas sighed. "It is getting worse." He reached into his pocket, pulling out his phone. "I can't figure out why they didn't search us."

"That is bizarre. Do they not know what they're doing or did they do that on purpose?" Taran puzzled away at that thought.

"I think that they did it on purpose. If we had used it before, we likely would have been moved somewhere quickly and where no one could find us." Thomas paused as he stared at his phone. "Who do I call?"

"Your family? Your employer?" Taran was trying to be helpful. She just didn't know what Thomas did. "What do you do for work, anyway?"

—

"Me? I'm a member of a security team." He grinned as she stared at him, astounded at his words.

"A security team member and you were abducted?" Taran shook her head. "That doesn't happen in real life."

"Unfortunately, it does. It happened to a friend on the team. Paul and his lady, Payten, went through some bad stuff just recently. And I have friends on two other security teams that went through things."

"They did? So, these security teams? They're that good?" Taran hid her smile even though her eyes sparkled with mischief.

Thomas stared at her before his eyes narrowed as he caught the sparkle in her eyes.

"We're that good. It's just that when ladies are in danger, we have to walk in. And on one of the teams, the one with two ladies, they had to step in to save their guys." He grinned as the smile broke out on her face.

"I see. Then, I suggest that I need to meet all these people and talk to them. Now, who are you going to call?"

"Don, my boss, I think. He'll round up the team and bring them in. I know it's Saturday and they're not working. But it's what we do. We take care of one another. And we will take care of you, Taran. I don't understand why I was abducted. And you? Was it just because you were there? Or is it related to your work as a pharmacist?" Thomas watched as Taran thought through his words.

"It could be either. I don't know that I have any enemies. I mean people were angry with me that I could graduate with my degree at age 19." She nodded as he shot her a surprised look. "I went to college at age 16 and graduated early. I've worked at that pharmacy since I graduated. I'm in the process of purchasing it if you must know."

"And that could play into it. Someone might not want you to purchase it. Perhaps they were waiting for you, saw me, and decided that I might come to your rescue if I saw what was happening."

Taran shrugged, knowing that was a possibility.

"I know the owner but I think that we need to look into that more. Your team can help?"

"They can. And I have other friends that can as well. They'll help us out at no cost, just as friends."

"Okay, then. Call or text your friends. I want to go home." Taran looked away, her emotions raw for a moment. She didn't want Thomas to see the tears that she was trying hard to control.

Thomas gave a sigh and wrapped an arm around her, snugging her tight to him. His chin rested on her head for a moment before he reached for his phone, sending off a text message to his team and also Aidan. They would find them, he knew. They just needed to stay hidden until then.

Chapter 6

Sighing in frustration, Don reached for his phone. The text messages had been coming in incessantly for the last hour or so. He was meeting with his team in an attempt to determine just where they could search for Thomas and Taran. He missed Thomas there. Thomas was one of the quieter ones on the team but he thought long and hard about situations. Many times, a simple comment from him had changed the course of their protective services with clients. Now that Don was looking at transitioning to training, Thomas would be an integral part of the team, just as the others would.

Moving away from the conversation among the other four, Don pulled out his phone, bringing up the last text message. He stared at it in shock, wiping at his eyes before he looked back at it. It was Thomas, simply stating where Taran and he were hiding. Don raised his head, finding Caleb watching him.

Caleb was on his feet, heading for Don. The other three looked around in surprise, saw the look on Don's face, and were also on their feet, heading for their team leader.

"Don? You have a stunned look on your face." Caleb stopped in front of him.

"I do?" He held up his phone. "This text? It's from Thomas. He's free and is hiding downtown with Taran. He hasn't given many details, but we need to organize and go in and get him." He glanced down at his watch. "It's mid-afternoon. He wants us to wait until dark if we can."

"And we need to talk to Aidan." Mark shared a look with Paul, knowing how that would go over.

"We do. For now, I'll just let him know that I have a line on his whereabouts. We'll get them safe, back here, and then call in Aidan."

"The street people. They moved in to help." Joshua was confident in his words. "It's not the first time that they have helped out."

"No, it's not." Paul rubbed at his cheek. "So, Don, what do we need to do to prepare?"

Don gave a few quick instructions, knowing that he didn't need to give many. The team worked together as a unit, without many words needed among them. It was how the team had developed.

Dusk found the five moving rapidly but quietly through the downtown area. Don nodded as he caught the eye of a man who seemed to be one of the most down-and-out characters on the street. He knew for a fact that it was an undercover officer.

Paul's hand went up to stop the group. They studied the building in front of him before Don and Paul headed for it. The other three took up positions outside where they could keep watch, praying in the meanwhile that Thomas and Taran were indeed in there and unharmed.

Don's phone was out as he sent a quick text to Thomas. He waited, knowing full well that Thomas would have received it and was assessing the safety of the two leaving their hiding place. A small scraping sound came to their ears before they moved forward.

Thomas appeared, Taran with him. He didn't let go of her hand as they moved rapidly out, sandwiched between Don and Paul. The other three men moved in to surround them as they emerged from the building. Settling down into the large van, Thomas wrapped an arm around Taran, keeping her close to him. He simply shook his head at the looks that he was being given.

"Don? Is Daci around?" Thomas asked after Don's sister.

"She can be." Don studied the two before he nodded, a text message to his sister asking her to bring some clothes and whatnot for Taran. "She'll meet us at my place. We're heading there for now."

Aidan stared at the text message that Don had just sent him, wonder on his face, praise on his lips before he was on his feet. Finding Toryn just heading towards him, he pointed towards Toryn's office.

"Aidan?" Toryn waited patiently for Aidan to speak.

"Don just sent a text message. They have Thomas and Taran."

"They do?" Somehow, this did not surprise Toryn. "Where are they heading?"

"To Don's. It's the safest place for now. He's reaching out to Thomas' family. We still haven't been able to contact Taran's." Aidan was frustrated at that

---

but understood how it was when one traveled in foreign countries.

"We'll keep trying. Head over there. Take their statements and then find me. I'm stuck here for now on paperwork." Toryn was frustrated at that. His day had been taken up in meetings. Somedays, he wondered why he had taken on the role of police chief but knew that he was where God had placed him.

Daci turned from where she had been watching through the front window for Don. She had set the bag with lady's clothing in a spare room, not sure why Don had asked that. She sighed to herself, something that she felt that she was doing a lot of. Thomas and Taran must be heading here. That was the only explanation that she could come up with.

Don headed for the office, intent on calling Titus and then the parents. Instead, he turned as he heard Titus' surprised voice greeting Thomas. He headed back that way, finding Titus and his parents standing there, wonder on their faces.

"We need to let them clean up, folks. Rose? If you would work with Caleb on a meal? I'm sure that these two are hungry. Aidan is on his way as well. We need them to give their statements before we ask for too many details."

Daci simply hugged Taran and then drew her away from the group, closing the bedroom door behind her.

"Here you go, Taran. I know that we've met at church. You have been someone that I have wanted to get to know better." Daci grinned at her new friend.

—

Taran smiled in return. She had watched Daci over the years, not sure if she should approach her or not.

"I would like that. Now, you've brought clothing for me, haven't you?"

"I have. I hope I made the right choices. I have a stack of clothing that was meant for the shelter. I just raided that pile."

Taran stared down at the clothing. It was not what she would have chosen but then again, her tastes were very conservative. She understood suddenly that her choices had been her mother's choices .

"You know, I think you've done well. I need to change my style. I've been dressing too old for me. This is perfect. Thank you. You are a blessing from God." Taran reached to hug Daci. "There's a shower attached?"

"There is. That door there." Daci pointed to one of the doors. "I expect that Don will want you two to stay here overnight. I'm staying. I have a room set up here for myself. Don insisted on that. I know that Aidan will want to speak with you. Let me pray with you first."

"God was there, Daci. He protected and defended us through this all. I was so worried about Thomas overnight. Now that we're free, we'll go our separate ways once tomorrow comes." Taran turned away to gather up clothing and headed for the ensuite bathroom, the door shutting quietly behind her.

Daci stared at the closed door for a moment before her head began to shake. *Thomas is not walking away from her, is he, Lord? I can tell by the way that he watches and looks at her that he's found his lady. Just like our other friends. Thank you for protecting them and bringing them home. Lead us to who was responsible for this and soon.*

Chapter 7

Aidan tucked his paperwork away in his briefcase, his eyes on his hands as he did so. He was not sure what to think about the facts that he had been told. He also didn't like it that they could not give much of a description of their attackers, even from that morning. The sunglasses and the hoodies this morning precluded that.

Thomas rose to his feet, stretching. His headache was improving now that he had been able to get medication for it. He was concerned, however, about Taran. How did he walk away from the lady who he was beginning to care about? He just didn't want to admit that to himself yet.

Don listened to Daci and Taran, nodding to himself. Daci was just taking Taran in as a friend. It's what she did, opening up herself to be friends with others. This did place her at risk, Don had to acknowledge, but that was how his sister had always been. He turned as he heard footsteps approaching him.

"Don?" Toryn stood there. He had taken time to come and find his friends, not as the police chief, but as a friend.

"Toryn? You're here? Aidan was taking their statements." Don turned to head towards the office, Toryn's hand on his arm stopping him.

"It's okay, Don. I'm here as a friend, nothing more right now. They're okay?"

"I think so. Jasper is heading this way to assess them." Jasper was a physician and friend who would assess the two and leave a report for Aidan.

"That's good. Now, what can we do for them?" Toryn turned to find Taran near him. "Taran?"

"Toryn? I wasn't aware that you were here. I thought that you would be around at some point."

Toryn grinned at her. There really wasn't that many years separating the group. Toryn had become police chief at a younger age than most.

"I am, Taran. How are you?" Even with a smile still on his face, his keen eyes studied her.

"I'm okay, Toryn. Just worried about Thomas. He was out of it for most of yesterday. I know that he has a headache. I'm worried that he has a concussion."

"We'll have him assessed. You weren't hurt at all?" Toryn watched her closely.

"No, I wasn't. I just don't understand it at all." Taran walked away, looking for Thomas who stood waiting to wrap her into a hug.

Titus stood near Daci, a frown on his face. He wasn't sure what was going on. All he knew was that his brother was back and all he could do was thank God that he was.

"Have they said anything, Daci?"

"No, they haven't. I didn't think that they would, given that they just gave their statements. Aidan is off shortly, so I suspect that Thomas will talk then. Come

—

on. Let's go help your mom find something to eat. I think I heard that your father was grilling."

Titus gave a grin.

"That he was. And Mom was working on salads, I think that she said." Titus reached to hug his friend, walking away from her and towards his brother.

Daci watched him walk that way before she turned to Taran, finding Taran just standing in the centre of the room, a lost look on her face. Moving to stand beside her, Daci nudged her with her shoulder.

"I don't know about you but there are times that I feel very overwhelmed with all the guys in my life. They tend to hover." Daci grinned at her.

Rose, who had come to find the two, began to laugh.

"Ain't that the truth, Daci. We both have that. Payten does as well. And so will Taran." Rose reached to hug Taran, holding on a little longer as she felt the younger woman clinging a little bit longer than normal.

"I don't think that will happen." Taran didn't see Thomas standing nearby, his father's arm along his shoulders, watching Taran with his heart in his eyes.

"Son? Do we need to talk?" Thaddeus' voice caught at Thomas' ear.

"Dad? About what?" Thomas' gaze followed his father's to where Taran stood with Daci and his mother.

"About Taran? She's important to you already, son. I know that you won't want to hurt her. You take care of the ladies, even though you don't date. I suspect that is about to change."

"It might, Dad, and it might not. We shared an adventure that is now over."

"But it's not, Thomas. Not until we find out who abducted you two." Toryn had walked over to stand beside them. "For now, you two are connected, just like Paul and Payten were. We have to work through this and find the ones responsible."

"I get that. I just wish that it was different." Thomas sighed, not sure where to go or what to say. He turned and walked away, not seeing Taran watching him do that.

Taran turned and walked away, heading for the outdoors and then walking away from the house. Mark and Paul had exchanged a glance and then followed her.

"Taran?" Mark's voice stopped her in her tracks. "You want to go home?"

"I do. I need to." Taran fought her emotions, raw from what she had been through and the danger that she had faced. "I can't stay here."

"Come on, then. We'll take you to get your car and then follow you home." Mark's hand turned her towards her truck and then opened the door for her. Paul crawled into the back seat.

Taran watched as the two men searched her car before she took the keys back.

—

“It’s okay?”

“It is, Taran. Now, we’ll follow you home and walk through it for you. How is your security system?”

“Security system? I don’t have one.” Taran’s gaze shifted between the two men as they shook their heads. “That’s a problem.”

“It is, Tar4an. You do need to invest in one. I’ll pick up what I need and stop by tomorrow to install it.” Mark’s hand went up. “It’s okay. We need to do this. Toryn and Aidan would strongly suggest this. This is what we do for friends.”

“Is that what I am? A friend? Right now I feel as if I’m the one who put Thomas in danger.” Taran’s face was sober.

“We don’t know who brought the danger to whom. We will be working on it. And we have reached out to friends to help.” Mark shut her car door and headed back for his truck.

“She’s ready to run, Mark.” Paul was assessing the area around them even as he spoke.

“She is. She’ll try it. Thomas won’t let her. It’s like it was with you and Payten. She would have tried to run and you would have gone after her.”

Paul could do nothing but nod and then petition God to defend his friends.

Chapter 8

The next morning, Taran stood on her front porch, watching as Mark walked towards her, a grin on his face. She studied the bags and boxes that he was carrying.

"You look as if you're prepared." Taran tried hard to hide the smile on her face but had problems doing that. "Where's Thomas?"

"Good morning, Taran. And how are you this beautiful morning?" He stopped on the steps, set his packages down, and simply hugged her quickly. "And Thomas? He's on the way. He stopped to grab breakfast for us. I hope that you haven't eaten."

"No, actually, I haven't. I haven't been up for that long."

Mark studied the dark circles under her eyes.

"Did you get any sleep last night?"

"Some. Daci called in the middle of the night and prayed for me. That helped." Taran was troubled that she had done that.

"That's Daci. She takes care of her friends. And I can guarantee you are considered that by all of us." He looked around as he heard a truck. "And here is Thomas. Okay if I go inside?"

"Go ahead, Mark. Just do what you need to." Taran watched as Thomas walked towards her in his turn.

"Taran?" Thomas simply set the food bags down and wrapped her into a tight hug. He felt her hugging him back and was grateful that they were free. "Okay, darlin'?"

"I don't know, to tell you the truth. I'm not sure if I ever will be." Her voice was muffled against him. "How about you?"

"I'm okay. I've been cleared by the physicians. Now, what is Mark up to?" He turned her towards the house.

"I didn't have a security system. Mark found out last night and decided that he had to install one." Taran was troubled at that. She just knew that Mark wouldn't take any money for that.

"That's Mark. In fact, that's all of us. We look after our friends." His arm was around her as he picked up the bags of food with one hand.

"Is that what we are, Thomas? Friends?" She looked up at him, seeing something in his eyes that gave her pause.

"We are. I pray that we remain friends and that God protects us all." Thomas set the food down, hearing Mark whistling in another room.

Taran reached to sort out the food. She was grateful for Thomas and his caring. She just didn't think that it would go too far.

"Have you heard from your parents?" Thomas reached to make coffee for them.

"No, I haven't. I didn't expect to. They've been traveling now for a month and expect to be gone for

—

another few weeks. It's their dream trip, traveling through Europe and then Australia. I'm fine now." Taran refused to admit to herself that she did need her mother, even though her mother didn't seem to need her.

"We're here for you, Taran. All of us. You're part of our group now." Thomas grinned at her, his eyes rising to where Mark stood just outside of the kitchen, nodding at his friend's words.

"So, what did you decide to pick up this morning, Thomas?" Mark grinned at the two of them as he took his takeout package of food.

"Our usual. For Taran, I just got pancakes and back bacon. I hope that is okay." Thomas bit at his lip for a moment, not sure if he had ordered what she liked.

"That's fine, Thomas. I can live with that." She reached for mugs, finding them taken from her hands and then finding herself seated as the two men worked around with their coffee before they sat on either side of her. Taran stared at the table top as Thomas asked a blessing on their food. She blinked rapidly. *I have never had friends like this. I like this, Lord, but I am afraid. More afraid than I have ever been. How do we stay safe and find the ones responsible?*

Thomas watched her carefully even as they joked around. He appreciated the fine sense of humour that Taran had, although he had to admit that it was dark at times. He frowned for a moment and then nodded. He had seen that before in healthcare workers. They used dark humour themselves at times.

Mark helped clear away the debris from their meals before he walked back through Taran's house. He was ready to set up the system. He turned for a moment as he heard Thomas' voice teasing Taran and smiled. He's found his lady. Now all they had to do was to keep her safe. He prayed that they could.

Taran turned from washing her hands, drying them on a towel that she threw on the counter. Her eyes were on Thomas as he studied a message on his phone. Her eyes closed for a moment as she thought back to her dreams as a teenager. These were dreams that she had set aside as never coming true. She had given them to God, knowing that she was surrendering a deep dream of hers. Thomas was the image of the knight in her dreams. Was he for real?

Thomas looked up at that point, seeing a certain sadness mixed with hope on her face. *Lord, protect my friend. I don't know what we've gotten mixed up in, but You do. You have promised to protect us, to defend us, and to bring us through the storms of life. I fear for Taran, that the storms will buffet her greatly. And myself as well. Dear Lord, just keep her safe. That's all I ask. I have no idea what will happen in the future, but I don't want to lose my friend.*

Taran walked away at that point, hearing a tap at the door. She studied Aidan who stood there, a grim look on his face. Her own face paled.

"Aidan?"

"Inside, Taran. We need to talk. I see that Thomas is here." Aidan looked up to see Thomas standing behind her.

"Mark is too. He's installing a security system for me." Taran wrapped her arms around herself, shaking with sudden fear.

"He is? You didn't have one? When do you work next?" Aidan's thoughts were racing.

"Tomorrow. Sunday and all, it's what it is. When I finish off the purchase, I intend to close on Sundays. It's not right to be working on that day." Taran walked away, leaving the two men staring at one another and then at her.

Chapter 9

Aidan stared at her, not having known that fact. This was something that he should have been told and had not been. He was angry and frustrated.

"You're buying the pharmacy?" Aidan spoke, his words sharp as his emotions grew.

"I am. I take over next week. Is that a problem?" Taran stared at him, feeling Thomas just sweeping her into his arms and pulling her back against him. She felt safe in his arms, a fact that puzzled her greatly.

"We weren't aware of that fact, Taran. It could play into what happened." Aidan dropped his briefcase on the kitchen table, spinning to face her. He saw the shuttered look on Thomas' face. This is not what he had expected that day, to find the two men there. "And have Mark go over your store once you've taken possession of it. Upgrade your security."

"I plan on that. I want to revamp that whole thing. That's my plan anyway as soon as I take over on Wednesday." Her hands found Thomas', feeling his grip firm and steady, bringing comfort to her.

"Good. We'll search it for you as well, Taran, just as a precaution." Aidan stared her down, seeing just when she comprehended his words.

Taran paled at that, feeling Thomas tighten his arms around her. Mark had approached with a question but stood and waited patiently for Aidan to finish his discussion with Taran.

Thomas turned his head slightly, sensing Mark there. The two men exchanged glances before Mark turned and walked back to his work. He would do what he could without Taran's input but he really did need it.

Taran spun away from Thomas, needing time to think. She wasn't ready to have someone in her life but God seemed to have other ideas for her life. She didn't know who was after her and that scared her.

Thomas watched her walk away before he spoke. His voice was tight as he spoke.

"What didn't you say, Aidan? I know you well enough to know that you wanted to say more."

"There is. She needs to come back and talk with me. Will she?" Aidan sighed to himself. This was not how it was to go, he knew.

"She'll be back. She walks away to regain her control over her emotions." Thomas turned to watch for Taran, seeing her standing at the end of the hallway watching him in return. His hand went out and she almost ran to him to be caught tight in his arms.

Aidan watched the two, knowing that he was seeing a couple in front of him, not two separate people. He nodded to himself again.

Thomas simply hugged his lady tight to him before he turned her to Aidan.

"Aidan does need to speak with you, darlin'. And Mark has questions about the system that he's setting up. Who do you want to speak with first? It's your decision. We all back that." Thomas waited patiently. He could feel Taran relaxing against him.

"With Aidan, I guess. He has other places to be." Taran frowned at Aidan as he grinned at her.

"Actually, I don't, Taran. This is the last interview of the day. I'm off duty once I've spoken with you. Take your time. If you need to go and see what Mark is doing, I'm fine with that. I see that you have coffee on the go. I could use one and a chance to sit." Aidan did just that after he found a mug and filled it with coffee.

Taran stared at him before she turned and walked to where Mark was waiting in her office. The two men could hear the quiet conversation between them.

"How are you, Thomas?" Aidan's question brought Thomas' head around.

Thomas nodded, knowing that Aidan was asking in both the capacity of an investigator and as a friend. He reached for his own mug of coffee, sitting down across the table from Aidan.

"I'm getting there, Aidan. The swelling is down but the bruise will take a while. I still don't understand it." Thomas had discussed the situation in detail with his team and also his family. No one could give an answer except for Titus. "Titus had an interesting statement. He thought that maybe someone had recognized me from my work, saw Taran drive in, and thought that I was there to protect her."

Aidan's eyes kept steady on Thomas even as his thoughts raced. That was something that he had briefly discussed with his supervisor and then with Toryn. They had set it aside as not probable. But he had to question if that had been the right decision. He would certainly look into that.

"What connection do you have with her other than this and church?" Aidan reached for his pen.

"I don't know that we do. I hardly ever go to a pharmacy. The only reason I did was for my neighbour. Is she the connection?" Thomas rubbed at the bruise on his face, worried that Mrs. Wright would become a target, just because of what he had done.

"Not that we are aware of. It's more likely one of the two of you are." Aidan reached for his phone, feeling its incessant vibrating. He read the text message and then accessed his email. Emma Finlay was at work, he noted, a friend who had a business of investigation and who could find people and places and things that no one else could.

Taran hesitated as she approached the kitchen, her thoughts on what Mark had discussed with her. He was correct, she knew. She had to upgrade all the security at home and in the building. She just didn't want to and that was a problem. Her eyes sought the ceiling as she prayed for peace in the turmoil, asking for the storm to be calmed. If the storm could not be calmed, then she asked that she be calmed. She had no other way to pray.

Thomas stood in the kitchen doorway, his eyes on her. He waited patiently for her, knowing that she was troubled but not knowing how to resolve it for her. He had had a long discussion with Don that morning.

—

The team was away next week on an assignment, leaving Monday morning and not back until Saturday afternoon. Thomas hated that he had to leave his lady and that Paul had to leave Payten. He prayed for his team, knowing that it was only God who protected them.

Chapter 10

Wednesday found Taran staring at the set of keys in her hand at the end of the day. She was now a pharmacy owner, not just a pharmacist working for someone else. It was a dream come true. She wanted her parents there to share the joy. That was what they had planned but the decision of the owner to sell had come up so quickly. Taran frowned at that. George Downs was not planning on selling so quickly. He had not explained his decision to Taran, simply helped her to buy the building and his business.

Aidan walked towards Taran, finding her turning towards him, fright momentarily on her face. He was no closer to knowing who had kidnapped Thomas and her. That worried him. The police force could not protect either one of them, particularly Taran, if they didn't find out who or why.

"Aidan? Is something wrong? You're here?" Taran became very worried. "Oh, no! It's Thomas! He's been hurt."

Aidan's hands on her upper arms stopped her words and had her pausing in her agitation.

"No, as far as I know, he's fine. He's with his team and they'll look after him. It's you that I'm here for. I wanted to be one of the first to congratulate you on your dream." Aidan nodded at the store. "You've accomplished it." His grin caused her to smile widely.

—

"I did. Thank you, Aidan, for being here." She looked past him. "And here are Daci and Payten. Ladies?"

The two ladies reached to hug her before hugging Aidan.

"We knew that this is a special day for you. We wanted to be part of it. So we invited ourselves to a party for you. Aidan, you're invited too."

"A party? That sounds like fun." Aidan grinned even wider. "And I can guess at Ben's."

"Of course. They want to be part of it." Payten grinned back as she linked an arm with Taran. "We're here as friends but also stand-ins for our guys. Come on, Taran. Let's party."

Taran began to laugh even as she heard her phone chime. Excusing herself, she pulled it from her purse. Her face softened as she saw a photo of Thomas, a sad look on his face, before she read his message just congratulating her and wishing that he could be there. He also asked her out on the weekend. The message ended with icons of flowers and red hearts.

Daci watched her face closely and nodded. *Thomas,* she thought. *He's been in touch. They're good for one another, just as Paul and Payten are so suited.*

Aidan followed Taran home that night, walking through her house and then around the perimeter. Word had reached them early that afternoon that another attempt would be made to kidnap her. They just had no idea why. He warned her to be extra careful as he walked away, not sure that she would. Today, she was on cloud nine, as they say, and he knew that she would not necessarily be careful.

The man watching her house from next door frowned sourly. He had been ordered to kidnap her once more. Only, there didn't seem to be an opportunity at all. She was too closely watched. He hesitated before he walked away. He would try again tomorrow.

Saturday, Don watched as his team tidied away their equipment, with easy quips, laughter, and teasing amongst themselves. It had been an easy assignment for a change, their protected person grateful for their help. His eyes settled on Thomas as he worked away with a grin on his lips but a frown appearing briefly every once in a while. Daci had been in touch, just updating him on Taran. She was safe, Daci said, but missing Thomas.

Thomas paused as he walked through the building, his steps slowing to a stop beside Don.

"Don? You're puzzled."

"I am, Thomas." Don looked around before he pointed to the door. "You're wanting to get cleaned up and head to find Taran. We'll talk on Monday. We have our weekly meeting that morning. I have news that I want to share with you."

"Good news, I hope." Thomas had been praying that they no longer took assignments. It was wearing them out. Now that he had a lady in his life, he didn't want to be away from home for days on end.

Don grinned. Thomas was asking but not asking, a habit that he had.

"You'll like it. This was our last days-long assignment. We're training from now on or only doing day assignments." Don's grin widened as Thomas almost let out a yell and then pumped his fist in the air. "I think I made a mistake. You don't want that."

Thomas' laugh broke out as did Don's.

"I'm glad, Don. I won't say anything to the others. That's your privilege. I know that's what you've wanted to do."

"It is, Thomas. We've done our share. I've conferred with both Abe and Richard. We each can fill a niche area, given our training and experience. We'll overlap in some ways but be fresh and new in others. Go on. Find your lady."

Thomas waved as he ran for his truck. He didn't see the truck following him closely, pulling away from him as he slowed to turn into his driveway. Quickly cleaning up and changing, Thomas headed for the florist where a friend worked. Picking up the roses that he had ordered, Thomas hesitated, his eyes on them before he looked at the store next door. A quick nod of his head happened before he headed there.

Taran turned as she heard Thomas' whistle. She tilted her head for a moment before nodding. He was happy, she decided. And that made her happy. She walked eagerly into his arms, feeling his hug tighten and then a kiss on her forehead.

"You're back!" She moved away from him, his flowers in her hands. Finding a vase, she arranged the roses, turning back to find Thomas standing beside her.

"I am. I am glad to be back. And I have news. We're not doing any more days-long assignments. Don let me know that today."

"You're not? Oh, that's what I've been praying. That's wonderful news!" Taran moved back into his arms, her own hug tight around him.

"It is. Now, I would like to take you out for a meal. Not at Ben's this time. At the little Italian restaurant. We need to celebrate." Thomas simply continued to grin at her.

"We do?" Taran was puzzled at that. She had spent a week feeling watched and uncomfortable when she was out and about.

"We do. You've found your dream. I'm not traveling any more. We have lots to celebrate. If it's okay with you, Mom asked if we could come for lunch tomorrow." Thomas waited for her to speak. He didn't want to rush her into a decision

"I would like that. Your mother and brother have both kept in contact over the week. Your father dropped in on Wednesday with a beautiful bouquet from them, just to congratulate me on my purchase. They are so sweet."

They walked out to Thomas' truck, not paying attention to who or what was around them. Neither of them saw the truck that pulled away from the curb and followed them. Mrs. Wright did and called Aidan,

—

simply giving the information to him. Aidan sighed. This was what they expected to happen and had prayed wouldn't.

Chapter 11

Taran walked slowly through her store on the Monday morning. She was the first one in that day and just wanted to savour the moment, as it was described at times, of being a business owner. She was still unsure as to the step, it had happened so quickly. But it had been something that she had prayed about and that her parents had prayed for.

Her father had finally reached out to her. They were on their way home, he stated. Was she well? They had been overly concerned in the last couple of weeks. She had simply told him that they needed to talk and that she had become involved in a danger of some kind. He had prayed for her, his words and father concern wafting across the airwaves to her. Taran was glad that they would be home that day. She needed them right now. She also wanted them to meet Thomas, who was becoming a huge part of her life.

Turning as she heard the door lock open and then click closed, Taran peered around a shelf and drew a deep breath of relief. The other pharmacist stood there, a grin on his face.

"Taran? You're here. How does it feel to be the owner?" Joe grinned at her as he passed her to find his locker in the break room.

"I'm still working on that." Taran grinned in return before she sobered. "It's just so strange that he wanted to sell so quickly. Did he say anything to you?"

—

Joe looked around the locker door, a frown on his face.

"No, he didn't. It took us all by surprise. He's young to retire." Joe shut and locked the door before he stood in front of Taran. "I'm glad that you've taken it over. I know that he has had offers that disturbed him. He hasn't said but I don't think that all of them were on the up and up."

"That's what I wondered. I'll have Aidan talk to George. There has to be a reason. Even a month ago, he was making plans for the store." Taran's voice died away as her face paled.

"Taran?" Joe was worried about his employer.

"That's when this all started, isn't it, Joe? What did I do?" Taran walked away, heading for her office. She sat in her desk chair, turning her phone around and around on the desk. She sighed at last, calling Aidan. Having to leave a voice mail for him was not what she wanted to do but what she had to.

By the afternoon, Taran was still waiting for Aidan to call her. She tried him again but still couldn't not reach him. She turned as she heard footsteps behind her as she was heading for the office to get ready to close for the day. Taran breathed a sigh of relief and simply moved into Thomas' hug.

"Okay, darlin?" Thomas could feel the tension in his lady.

"Not really. Let me lock up and then I can leave." Taran rapidly did the end-of-day tasks that needed to be done. She then reached for Thomas' hand

—

as she walked back towards the front of the store, set the alarm, and then locked the door. "We need to talk, Thomas. And I think that we need to talk with Don as well."

"We do? Then, how be we head that way? He was going to be home. The sooner that we talk with him, the sooner we can resolve this." Thomas followed her to her home, waited for her to change into casual clothes, and then drove off, heading for Don's. He slowed as he recognized Aidan's car heading his way, stopping beside his vehicle. "Aidan?"

"Thomas. And Taran. Taran, I got your messages. I was tied up and couldn't get back to you. We do need to talk." Aidan's voice was stern.

"We do. We're heading for Don's. Can you come that way?" Taran refused to have Thomas turn around. She was determined that she take back control of her life and her movements.

Aidan stared at her before he caught the look of amusement on Thomas' face. He frowned at him as Thomas simply shrugged and then drove off. Aidan sighed before he turned his car around to follow them. He was off the clock for now but had wanted to touch base with Taran. He could hear the fear in her voice as he had listened to her voice mail message.

Don stared around the front door as he saw Thomas and Taran walking towards him with Aidan trailing along behind him. This is not good was his thought. He simply pointed towards the kitchen. He had been about to grill some food and knew that he had

—

plenty for all four of them. Daci was working, he knew, and would not be around.

"Thomas? Didn't you just leave the building?" Don grinned at him.

"I did. We need to talk. Taran has something to discuss with us. But you were getting your meal ready." Thomas felt bad about disturbing Don's meal.

"I have plenty, Thomas. That is not a problem." Don studied Taran, seeing the distraught look that she was trying to hide. "Can she wait?"

"I can, Don. I'm not sure that it is important, but a fact was brought to my attention today and I think that we need to discuss it." Taran moved past him into the kitchen, ready to help prepare the meal.

Aidan came to a stop beside Thomas, a questioning look on his face.

"What's this all about?" Aidan kept his eyes on Taran.

"I'm not sure. She was upset to some extent when I found her this afternoon. I don't know why. She was alone in the store when I got there. I'm not sure if that's such a good idea at this point." Thomas was frustrated, not able to be with Taran all the time but wanting to be.

"You should just marry her, Thomas. That would solve part of the problem." Aidan walked away, not seeing the look on Thomas' face.

I could do that, couldn't I, Lord? I could marry Taran and try my best to protect her. But neither one of us is ready for that. It has to be in Your time and

Your will. This lady is special to me in a way that no other lady is.

Taran stopped in front of Thomas, searching his face, finding a look in his eyes that puzzled her. It said that she was cherished and special and loved. Thomas simply swept her into a hug, a kiss dropped on her forehead.

Chapter 12

Aidan helped to clear away the debris of their meal, his eyes shifting to Taran. He could tell that she was upset and trying to hide it. He sighed. He didn't know the lady well enough to judge just how she was feeling or what was wrong. His gaze then shifted to Thomas, finding that man with his eyes on the lady. Aidan could see Thomas' heart in his eyes and looked away.

"Taran? What happened today?" Aidan finally spoke up, knowing that something had. He pulled out a chair at the kitchen table, waiting for Taran to speak.

Taran reached for Thomas' hand, her eyes on Aidan. She was unsure how to proceed now. Thomas shared a look with Don and then began to pray. Taran felt herself beginning to relax, feeling God calming the storm within her.

Raising her head, Taran kept her eyes on Aidan, knowing that she had to speak but not wanting to place any blame on George.

"Taran?" Aidan waited patiently for her to speak.

"It's about the drugstore, Aidan. George told Joe that he suddenly decided to sell in the last month. I knew that he wanted to sell at some point but not this quickly. I'm afraid now that something was off about it. Did I do something wrong?" Taran rubbed her hands together, not sure what to say. "He offered it to me. I took his offer. He did help me secure the

---

financing that I needed through our bank. What Joe said today? That makes me wonder if there was a reason why he suddenly decided to sell. Can you determine that?" Taran raised her eyes to gaze at the ceiling. "I wanted to do this at some point. When George offered me the business at a really good price, I prayed about it and felt that I had permission to go ahead. Now, I'm doubting myself."

"That's a good question, Taran. We wondered what his thoughts were. I'll talk to him tomorrow." Aidan had been avoiding his phone vibrating but the incessant vibrating had him on his feet and excusing himself. He walked away and pulled out his phone, an inaudible sound coming from him. He returned to the kitchen just to excuse himself and then left.

Toryn turned as Aidan approached, shaking his head at the detective. This crime scene was not what they had expected. It was a horrible scene with blood staining many objects and the house tossed.

"Toryn? It's George?" Aidan was shocked as he stared around at the scene.

"It is. It happened in the last couple of days, the medical examiner has indicated." Toryn had been in the neighbourhood when the call came in. He was not on duty but given that there was an ongoing investigation, he had stopped at the scene and stood back watching what was happening.

"It was? It's bizarre, you know. I just was meeting with Taran. She said that Joe, the other pharmacist, had told her that morning that George just decided quickly to sell. She was surprised at that and feels that she has walked into something else." Aidan rubbed a finger at a temple. He was starting with a headache.

"He did? That doesn't sound like George. He's been a staple in this community for a number of years. When did she discover that?"

"Today from what she said. She's worried that she's stepped into something that she shouldn't have." Aidan watched as the techs worked around the scene. "They'll be a while."

"They will be. I'm off. Call me with any details that you find out. And about Taran? She probably has. You'll need to investigate George now." Toryn walked away, knowing that Aidan would be doing just that.

Aidan walked away himself many hours later. He glanced at his watch. It was now early morning and he was exhausted. He headed for the office, knowing that he had to but wanting instead to head for home and his bed. He reached for his phone, scrolling through his messages and stopping at the one from Taran. *Taran, what did you just go and do? What did you find that you shouldn't have?*

Taran turned from her office desk the next afternoon, heading out to work behind the counter filling prescriptions. Her mood was somber. Aidan had stopped by briefly that morning, just to inform her that George Downs had been murdered and ask her what she had become involved in. Did she even know?

She had been unable to reach out to Thomas. Thomas was busy training as was his team members.

Taran looked up for a moment and saw Daci and Don walking her way. She paled, immediately thinking that something had happened to Thomas.

"It's okay, Taran. Thomas is fine. He just asked if we could hang around here until you finished work. He's tied up with what he's working on." Don grinned at her before he headed to the small coffee area that she had incorporated into the store.

"He scared me, Daci. Does he know that?" Taran's heart began to beat regularly again.

"We know. We need to talk and talk tonight, Taran. We'll be around for now. If you need us, call us." Daci moved away to browse the store, her eyes watchful as she did so.

Don turned from where he had stopped, feeling eyes on him. He couldn't see anyone other than the other pharmacist who looked down when Don turned. He frowned. Joe was someone that they were looking into and it wasn't good what they were finding. Thomas had reached out again to Emma, giving her the new details of the last day. She had not been surprised, she said, and promised to be back with information as soon as she could.

Taran locked up, Don watching the area around the building. They had had word that someone was determined to abduct Taran once more. Aidan had reached out to his team, asking for his help. For now, Taran was under their protection. He just didn't know how she would react. Thomas had been disturbed, he knew, wanting to be with his lady, but knowing that he couldn't.

"Don? There is more to that than just being here to watch me lock up." Taran stared at him and then at Daci.

"Where are your car keys, Taran?" Don reached for them, pointing towards Daci's car. "You're with Daci. I need to search your vehicle." He walked away, leaving Taran staring after him.

Taran's mouth snapped close before she turned to Daci. Daci had a sympathetic look on her face.

"Come on, Taran. Let's get you out of the open and into my car. Don will drive yours home once he's searched it. The guys are here." Daci nodded towards the trucks now surrounding Daci's vehicles.

"They are? What happened? Something has. I know that George is dead. Aidan called me quickly this morning." Taran fastened her seatbelt, her eyes meeting those of Thomas, who gave her a brief smile.

"There has been. I'll let Don explain it but you are not safe, Taran. Not at all." Daci drove away, the men's trucks surrounding her vehicle as much as possible. "I'm heading for Don's. For now, that's where you'll be." Daci shook her head as Taran's mouth opened to protest. "Aidan asked for that."

Chapter 13

To say that Taran was frustrated was an understatement. She had simply walked into Don's house and to the bedroom where she flopped down on the bed. She was exhausted, her sleep disturbed by dreams and nightmares.

Thomas had watched her walk away, Daci standing beside him. Her arm wrapped around his for a moment before she walked away. The men on Don's team were like brothers to her. She cared deeply about them and what was going on with them. Thomas had turned at last, walking away to do what he needed to do.

Don appeared at last, Aidan following him. This was not how they had planned their afternoon and evening. Paul had had plans with Payten and Don had sent him on his way. For now, they would be working in pairs in eight-hour shifts to protect Taran and also Thomas. It was what they needed to do.

Aidan turned from the door that he was staring through. He needed to talk to Taran but she seemed to be avoiding him. This had to stop, he decided.

"Daci? Can you find Taran? I need to speak with her and now." Taran would not back down from her running from him.

Taran turned from where she was seated on the bed. She had showered and changed but just didn't want to face the men. She felt ashamed and threatened, not by them but by whoever it was that was after her.

This had to stop, she knew. Daci sat beside her, an arm wrapped around her friend.

"Taran? What's wrong?" Daci's voice was quiet, not sure how to approach her friend.

"I don't know. I feel ashamed, I guess. Somehow, I've become involved in something that has involved Thomas and the team. They shouldn't be. I just know that one of them will be hurt and hurt badly." Taran swiped at the tears that trickled down her face.

Daci began to pray for her friend, knowing that was about all that she could do for her.

"They don't look at it like that, Taran. They want to do everything that they can to help keep you safe and keep Thomas safe. I can tell you one thing. Thomas is not walking away from you. He's treating you differently from any other lady. He doesn't bring flowers to ladies, not like he has with you. He's ready to settle down, get married, and if God wills, have a family. He has chosen you, Taran."

Taran nodded, knowing that Daci was correct. He had expressed that interest to her. They were both praying through that situation.

"I know that, Daci. It's just I feel that I am so dangerous."

"He won't look at it that way, Taran. But there's more." Daci waited for her friend to speak.

"There is. I just need my mom and dad. They're trying to find a flight but they can't for now. Where they are? There are not many commercial flights that go in and out. If I could find someone with their own plane, I'd hire them to go and get them." Taran rose at last, looking for Aidan but finding Thomas instead.

Daci watched as Thomas hugged Taran and then turned her to where Aidan was waiting. They could not put off that talk any longer. Finding Don, Daci simply made a request. Don listened and then nodded, walking away to the outdoors to find privacy as he reached out to a friend.

Taran sat beside Aidan, waiting for him to speak. She could tell that he was troubled. She just didn't know why.

"Taran? I have some bad news for you." Aidan didn't know how to approach her. "It's about George."

Taran nodded, thinking that she knew what he was about to say.

"George? Is he involved in something that I should know about? Did I do something wrong buying his business?"

"No, you didn't do anything wrong." Aidan shared a look with Thomas, who simply stared back, an inscrutable look on his face. "I was on a crime scene today. It was at George's home. When is the last time that you spoke with him?" Aidan's notebook and pen were out, ready to make notes.

"George? What happened? When did I last speak with him? Last Saturday. He called, just to see if everything was going all right. Come to think of it, he didn't sound like himself. He had a tone in his voice that I'd never heard before. If I had to define it, I would

---

say that it was fear." Taran felt Thomas' arm around her before she leaned into him.

"I see. Today, I was called to his house. I'm sorry, Taran. He was killed sometime in the last couple of days. A neighbour called it in to use after he hadn't seen George for a few days and asked for a welfare check."

Taran paled, feeling Thomas' arm tighten around her.

"Murdered? But who? And why?" Taran's voice was barely a whisper. "Does it involve the pharmacy?"

"That's one angle that we're looking at. I'll have an plain-clothes offer on site for the next few days, just to watch out for you. I am asking for a search warrant to go back through the business records. That officer will be doing that as well as being there for you. I understand from Don that two of his team will be with you as well."

"He can't do that!" Taran was becoming agitated at the thought. "They have their own work to do."

"They do, but Don will do this. You're part of his family, Taran, whether you realize it or not." Aidan kept his eyes on Thomas, seeing the look that everyone else was beginning to see on his face. *He cares for her*, he thought. *We need to keep these two safe. I'm just not sure that we can.*

Thomas simply wrapped his other arm around Taran, seeing Don approaching them. His team had

—

74

talked, knowing that Don would want this, and decided who would work what hours.

"I have a friend who will step in if we need that. I have already spoken with Richard. His team is available during the day if we need to do that." Don sat on Taran's other side. "For now, we'll work with my team. I can work around keeping you safe and doing what we need to."

"I get that, Don. I just don't know why George would be killed." Taran's face paled even more. "For the drugs?"

"It could be. That is one thing that we're looking at. Now, what can you tell me about George? You've worked for him for a number of years."

"I have. It's difficult to know what to say. He was a private person for the most part. I don't know much about his personal life. As to the pharmacy? He approached me about a month ago, just when this all started, about buying the business. I agreed. Maybe I shouldn't have."

Chapter 14

A week had passed with Don's men guarding Taran. She had finally just told him to stop, that the men being there was not accomplishing anything other than the men losing sleep. He had nodded, knowing that she was correct. Thomas had not been happy but there wasn't much that he could say. He just had to support Taran in her decision.

Taran's parents had appeared the day after George's body had been found. Taran had opened her front door that afternoon, shock and happiness on her face. Her father had reached to hug her, hanging on tightly before he turned her to her mother.

Tam and Rachel had been surprised when two men had shown up at their hotel, simply stating that they were there to fly them home. Ian and Murphy, two members of Abe Finlazy's Rebel's Elite Security, had stated that Don had reached out to Abe and Abe had sent them on to find Taran's parents. She needed them home and that was what they were there to do.

"Mom? Dad? How?" Taran was surprised to see them. "I didn't think that you could get a plane out for a week."

"Apparently you have friends with a plane. A couple of gentlemen from a security force showed up and brought us home. We are grateful for that." Rachel stood with an arm around her daughter. "I hear that you are having an adventure."

Taran snorted, causing her parents to smile.

"If that's what you want to call it. I don't." She sighed, knowing that she had to come clean with her parents. "George was murdered a few days ago."

Tam turned from the counter where he had been pouring their coffees.

"Murdered? How?"

"I don't know. Aidan is not saying much. And it has not been in the news very much. Aidan said that they would keep the details under wraps as he put it." Taran reached for the casserole that she had placed in the oven when she arrived home. "I'm scared, Mom and Dad. I don't know how that affects me or the business. I think that I made a mistake in going ahead with the business."

Tam and Rachel shared a look. They both nodded, knowing that Taran was correct in her feelings but that she was also hurting.

"I don't know that you did, love." Tam reached for his ladies' hands, bowing his head to pray for Taran. When he finished, he raised his head, his eyes on his daughter. "We were surprised that it happened so quickly. Was George running from someone?"

Taran shrugged, not sure how to answer. She knew that George had been different in the last month that he had been the store owner, but she thought it was just giving up the business.

"I don't know, Dad. I really don't know. He was different. I just thought that it was because he was retiring. Maybe I was wrong. I don't remember anyone coming around that would have caused him to be afraid."

"It may have been outside of business hours. And it likely was." Rachel reached to squeeze her daughter's hand. "We're praying for you. And for Aidan as well as he investigates." She shared a look with Tam before she smiled, looking very much like her daughter. "Now, this man in your life?"

"Thomas? I thought that he would be here for a meal." Taran was on her feet, searching for her phone. She read the text from Thomas, a soft look on her face that caused her parents to share another look. "He's tied up with something but hopes to be here soon." She didn't see the second look that her parents shared, her parents seeing their daughter was falling in love.

Thomas turned in frustration from the desk in the office. He had planned to spend the evening with his lady. Only, a sudden search for a missing person had stymied that plan. He had gladly given up his time with his lady, knowing that was what she would have wanted him to do. He just missed her.

Don walked towards his team, finding his seat at the table. They had been able to pinpoint where the missing person was being held. That information had been passed on to the appropriate police force. They just needed to debrief before they could head home. It was late and he could see how tired his team was.

"Thanks, guys. This is what we do. And I think we just found a niche that we can work with. We'll pray about it." Don did just that, rising with his team and sending them on their way.

—

Thomas reached for his phone, scrolling through his messages. He stopped at the one from Taran, a pleased smile crossing his face. His phone hit his kitchen counter as he reached for bread and meat to make a sandwich. He wasn't really hungry but he did need to eat.

Taran turned from the front door, locking it after her parents. She had been very happy to see them and know that they were home safe. She just missed seeing Thomas. The chiming of her phone with his ringtone had her almost running to find it, seeing the text message that he had sent. A soft smile crossed her face.

The men watching both homes were frustrated. They were under orders to bring the two to their boss. Only that didn't seem to be happening. The couple was too closely watched. They would need to change their plans but they didn't know what to do. The pressure was growing on them.

Don walked back through his house, his thoughts on the day. The missing person had been found and was now in the hands of the authorities, being kept safe somewhere. He had enjoyed the hunt and knew that his team had as well. Mark in particular had led in this, his specialty on the team that of investigations. He would have to sit down with his team once more and discuss where they were heading. Yawning, Don turned from the windows, not seeing the men watching his home and business.

Tam turned to Rachel as they tidied away their belongings. They had not spoken about their daughter, not yet.

—

"Tam? What has Taran gotten herself into?" Rachel finally turned to her husband, walking into his arms.

"I don't know. I fear for her, love. We need to meet this Thomas as well." Tam frowned for a moment. "I think I know who he is. He's one of Don's team, isn't he?"

"That's what she said. He's from our church. I don't know all the men there that well. I think I know who he is too."

"We'll pray for her and Thomas, love. That's all we can do. God is in control even when it seems that he isn't."

Chapter 15

Running for her car two days later, Taran frantically worked the key fob, praying that she reached safety. She could hear the heavy footsteps behind her, coming closer as she had to slow to reach for her car door. The door slammed behind her as she leapt inside, the doors locked behind her. The man stopped directly in front of her car, boxing her in.

Taran shoved the key into the ignition and started the car. She just didn't know where to go. A quick look behind her showed her that nothing was behind her. Shoving the car into reverse, she floored the gas pedal and shot backwards, swerving as she hit the road and then shoving the car into drive. She sped away, leaving the man running after her, rage on his face. He had been defeated that day but he would find Taran again and take her. That was a promise that he made to himself.

Slamming and locking the door behind her, Taran leaned back against it. She was deeply afraid and not just for herself. She was afraid for her staff. Did she need to close down her business and quit her dream? Taran prayed that she didn't have to but she knew it might come to that.

Thomas ran for Taran's door. He had not heard from her that day since her early morning text. That scared him. Caleb was beside him, Joshua and Mark searching the outside around her place.

Hammering at the door, Thomas shook the knob, his voice calling for Taran. He heard something hit the door on the inside before the knob turned under his hand and the door shot open from his shove. He simply gathered Taran to him, his arms wrapping tightly around her. Caleb walked rapidly through her home, searching for anything amiss. He stopped in her office, a frown on his face. Something was off there and he needed to clear the house so that the police could move in.

"Thomas? We need to leave. Something is off in here." Caleb's hand simply shoved at the two, forcing them through the door and towards cover in Thomas' truck. His hand snagged Taran's purse. He followed the pair, handing her the purse and then standing with his back to her truck door.

Joshua and Mark headed for them, questioning looks on their faces. They nodded at Caleb, heading back for the house and entering it.

Taran watched them closely, not sure why they had been rushed out of the house. Thomas stood in a way so that he could watch Taran and the area right around them. Caleb pocketed his phone, having reached out to Aidan. Aidan had simply sighed and promised to send some patrol officers. He wasn't able to get there at the moment.

The patrol officers walked through Taran's home and then the perimeter of it. Taran watched them closely, the window on the truck lowered somewhat. She turned as she heard another vehicle and saw Don approaching. She sighed. This had just gone from bad to worse. How did she manage to stay safe?

Don stopped as Caleb approached him, a stern, sober look on his face.

"Caleb? What's going on?" Don's gaze shifted between Caleb and Taran.

"Someone was in her home. Mark is pulling the video feed. It has to have been sometime after she left for work and before she came home. I could feel something off and rushed her out of the house. Aidan's not here but he's hoping to be shortly."

"In her home? I thought that we had the security really tight." Don rubbed at the back of his neck. This was not what he wanted to hear.

"We did. Whoever did this is watching her very closely. I asked her if she had been getting any parcels, letters, or text messages. She said no and then asked if she should be." Caleb gave a small smile at the look on Taran's face as she asked that.

"She should be. She's not here at home. Has she been at work?" Don walked towards Thomas' truck, nodding at Thomas as he did so. "Taran? Have you been receiving anything at work?"

"No, I haven't. Not at home, either. I should be, shouldn't I? Isn't that how they threaten you and cause you to do something stupid?" Taran rubbed at her upper arms, chilled for a moment.

"Normally, people under attack such as you are do receive these items. However, this is different. They're keeping that close an eye on you. I would hazard a guess one of them is watching this right now, ready to grab you and disappear with you. You need

—

to stay here in the truck until we walk you back through your house. I'm heading over there to see what I can find out." Don walked away before she could protest.

Thomas opened the back door of his truck, retrieving a blanket. He wrapped it around her and then stood with his back to the closed door.

"Thomas? What did Caleb find?" Taran's voice was subdued and barely audible.

"I don't know, Taran. He didn't say. But something had to be off for him to react that way. I know him too well." Thomas turned to wrap an arm around her before he began to pray for her.

His four team mates monitored the crowd that had gathered. They knew most of them by now with her neighbours coming over and introducing themselves. Paul's gaze was on one man, a stranger. He turned to speak with Joshua who nodded. He too had focused on that man. They walked towards him, finding him turning and walking rapidly away.

Paul and Joshua picked up their pace, their steps becoming running ones as they took off after him. Paul tackled him and took him down before he drew him to his feet. A hard grasp on the man's arms by Paul and Joshua had him returned to face a patrol officer.

Aidan approached, having caught the man's flight as he took off with the two men after him. A search of his pockets by a patrol officer turned up handcuffs, strips of cloth, and a weapon. Aidan took the wallet handed to him, his eyes on the man's face. He nodded to himself. He knew the man without even looking at the identification. That identification confirmed the man's identity.

Thomas had watched the activity, his arm still around Taran. He could feel her shifting on the seat, her own eyes on Aidan as he approached her.

"Taran? This man? He was here to abduct you. This activity around her kept that from happening. What did Caleb find in your house?" Aidan held out his phone. "This. It is a device that would have sent a shock through you, rendering you incapable of resisting anyone who tried to abduct you. They were in your home, Taran. We can't let you back in for now, not to stay. We'll walk you through to pack up what you need. Then we need to find somewhere safe to keep you."

"What about work, Aidan? Will they try something there?" Taran was afraid for her staff.

"They might. I have spoken with Toryn. There will be a patrol officer who will escort you from your vehicle and to your vehicle each day. They will also go through the building before you open and as you close. Your business is important to our town and that area. We don't want to see you close it down because of this." Aidan walked away at that, not letting Taran protest, even though he could tell that she wanted to.

—

Chapter 16

Another week had passed with Aidan no closer to finding out who was behind it all. The mystery of who had murdered George Downs also weighed on him. He knew that it was somehow connected to Taran but he had no proof of that. Taran had simply walked away from him the night before, not responding to his concern. Thomas had shrugged and walked after her. Aidan was frustrated with her attitude but he knew that she was worried and troubled and more than likely terrified.

Thomas had stopped at the store late that day. He had driven Taran to work and was now waiting for her to finish up. He nodded at the patrol officer who approached to walk through the building as Toryn had requested.

Taran locked up the building, thanked the officer, and then turned to walk into Thomas' arms. She was afraid that day, more than she had been. A text message had finally come through, threatening her. Taran knew that she needed to send it to Aidan. She was just afraid that he would decide to lock her away somewhere and throw away the key. Taran knew that she didn't want that.

Thomas reached for Taran's hand, knowing that something had happened that day. If she didn't tell him soon, then he would question her. At the moment, they were heading for her parents' home, invited to a meal as was his family. Thomas simply wrapped her into a hug before he opened the truck door and waited

—

for her to climb in. Once behind the wheel, he started the truck and waited for Taran to speak.

Taran drew in a deep breath. She had been in constant prayer about what to do the complete day. She withdrew her phone from her pocket and found the text message. She hesitated before she handed the phone to Thomas.

Thomas took it, his eyes on her. His heart hurt for his lady. This was not what he wanted to see on her face, the terror that she was feeling. His eyes dropped to the text before he drew in a deep breath. He simply forwarded the message to himself and his team and then on to Aidan. When he was done, her phone was handed back to her as he reached to wrap her into a hug.

"When did this come, darlin'?" He waited quietly for her to speak, knowing that she would eventually.

"This morning, just as I opened up. I didn't know what to do." Taran fought her terror once more, not realizing that tears were trickling down her cheeks. "I know that God is protecting me, Thomas. It just hurts to be told this. To be told that I would disappear and no one would ever see me again. Who does this?"

"Someone who means you harm. I can't be with you all the time, as much as I would like to be. We're not in a place where I would even ask you to marry me." Thomas didn't see the look of wonder on Taran's face.

"Thomas? What did you just say?" Taran shoved at him to make him sit back.

———

"That I would marry you to keep you safe? I do mean that, Taran. You are beginning to mean a lot to mean. I don't want to lose you." Thomas didn't look at her, his eyes on his hands. He saw Taran's hand as it reached for his.

"Thomas? Do you know what that means to me? To have someone say that? I would marry you, if you were to ask. We need to talk about this. Thank you."

Thomas raised his eyes, seeing the look on her face, a look that gave him hope that his growing feelings for her might just be returned. His hand rested on her cheek for a moment before he put the truck into gear.

"We'll talk, darlin'. But for now, we need to head for your mom's. Do you need to change?"

Taran shook her head, her eyes on the side mirror, watching as a car pulled out after them.

"No, I have some clothes at Mom's that I can use. I always leave something there in case I need it." Taran bit at her lip. "Are we being followed? That car pulled out behind us when you drove away."

Thomas looked into the rearview mirror and shook his head.

"It belongs to a friend, Taran. He's on the force here and decided to follow us today. It's okay. He's on his own time. I have a number of friends doing just that, keeping you safe." Thomas grinned at her.

"They are? And are they doing that for you too?"

Aidan stared at the text message that Thomas had forwarded to him. *It was starting*, he thought. *Now, how do we do this, Lord? How do we keep her safe and keep Thomas safe as well? He's going to be right there, taking care of her, and putting himself into danger. It's what we do for the ladies.*

He turned and walked from his office, heading for his supervisor's office. He sat down into a chair, waiting for his supervisor, Lyle, to turn from his computer.

"Aidan? You're troubled? Which case?" Lyle knew his detectives. He had made sure that he knew them well.

"Taran's. She's starting to receive the text message. Thomas forwarded one that she received. I'm not sure that she would have herself. It simply said that she would disappear." Aidan rubbed at his temple. He had a headache developing that he knew would just keep growing.

"I see. And this is the first that she has received?" Lyle sat back, puzzled as well that Taran had not received any messages.

"It is. I check with her each day. As soon as she sees it's me, her first comment is that no, she had not had any text messages or packages. She doesn't let me even say hello." Aidan grinned at that. "She has a wicked sense of humour buried right now."

"I know that she does. I know her parents and know Taran as well." Lyle leaned forward, a frown on his face. "So how do you do this? How do you find the ones responsible? And have you determined yet if it's connected to George?"

"It has to be, Lyle. George sold her the store. Joe did confirm with me that George decided to sell very quickly. He had not been acting as himself that last month. When I asked if Joe thought that George was afraid, he just looked at me for a moment. His comment was that he had not thought of that but looking back, he was sure that George was. He could not determine just from whom or why. Given the nature of the store, there were always people in and out of it." Aidan frowned as he remembered his conversation with Joe.

"And that makes it difficult to determine who might have been there as a threat. It is likely someone who is a townsperson, male or female. Now, what can we do to go ahead with that?" Lyle reached for a pad of paper and a pen.

Aidan looked at him and nodded. This was what he had expected from Lyle. Now, he was ready to talk and talk he did. Lyle nodded, made notes, and asked questions when he needed to. At last, Aidan sat back, a look of surprise on his face. An hour had passed while he was speaking. He reached for his bottle of water, sipping at it, as he waited for Lyle to digest what he had said and then to speak.

Lyle looked up at last, nodding at Aidan. They had made progress, he decided. His words to Aidan were concise as he repeated certain details. Aidan looked at him in surprise. He hadn't realized that he had come to a conclusion, right or wrong. It was now up to him to decide how to proceed. Lyle watched Aidan, nodding again.

"Now, where do you head, Aidan?" Lyle asked the question that really didn't need to be asked.

"I need to speak with Taran and Thomas again. I also need to talk to both their families, his team mates, and George's family. I also have to go back to the store and talk to the employees. I'm not looking forward to that. Taran is very protective of her staff."

"And she is right to be like that. Now, off with you. Set aside the work for the weekend. You're off and need that time. Find something fun to do." Lyle grinned as Aidan nodded and then rose, walking away from the office and finding his car.

Aidan stood for a moment, his face turned to the sky, his eyes closed. He felt the soft breeze that caressed his face, his heart raising in prayer for his friends.

—

Chapter 17

Tam watched his daughter closely that night, a frown on his face as he did so. Something had happened, he could tell, and she didn't want to tell them. He would approach after their meal and draw her aside to talk with her. Only, Tam figured that Thomas would want to be part of that conversation.

Thomas watched as Taran tried her best to interact with their families. She was struggling, he saw, and drew her away to a corner where they could have privacy. Wrapping her into his arms, he waited for her to relax. He could see their families watching them.

Titus frowned before he turned to their father.

"Dad? What happened today?"

Thaddeus shrugged, not sure what was going on.

"I don't know. I think something did. They'll tell us when they're ready." Thaddeus turned as Tam stopped beside him. "Tam?"

"I would say that she received something that has really rattled her. She's not normally like this." He sighed. "But then again, she's never gone through anything like this." Tam walked towards the couple, Thomas watching him do so. "Taran? Talk to us. Tell us what happened."

Taran looked up at Thomas who had turned his head to look at her. He nodded. He knew that she did have to tell her family. They were threatened and needed to take precautions.

Taran sighed, knowing that she did have to speak. She hated that the difficulty and danger that she faced had now come to her family.

"I received a text message this morning, Dad. It threatened to abduct me and make me disappear. And it threatened my family and friends." Taran didn't look around, not wanting to see the look on her family's faces or on the faces of Thomas' family. She could hear the indrawn breaths from everyone.

Titus stalked over to stand beside Thomas, a hand on Taran's shoulder.

"Taran? You have spoken to Aidan?" He waited for Taran to respond.

Thomas sighed himself. He knew that Taran was not going to answer that.

"She hadn't. She received the text this morning. I sent it on to Aidan when I picked her up from work. He'll look into it." Thomas raised his eyes, meeting those of Titus. "We need to discuss this but I'm not sure what we'll do. It's not like what I do. We go in and protect those we have to. We don't look into things. That was, we didn't until Paul. I know that the guys are doing that."

"And what about Emma?" Rose approached the couple, an arm around Taran.

"I've been in touch with her. She's been tied up on some really urgent investigations as can happen. She'll work on it as she can." Thomas gently turned

Taran to face their families. "They're concerned about you, darlin'. We'll discuss it tonight now that they know what you received."

"I hate this, Thomas. It shouldn't have got to this." Taran raised a hand to wipe away a tear from her cheek. She refused to let any more fall.

"It always does, darlin'. It always does. Now that they know, they can take precautions. If we hadn't told them, then they would not have been watching out for themselves." Thomas moved away as Rachel moved in to hug her daughter.

Titus frowned for a moment before he headed for the door, knowing that the others had not heard the soft tap at the door. Aidan stood there, dressed in jeans and a T-shirt.

"Aidan? You're here?" Titus shut the door after Aidan entered. "Have you eaten yet?"

"No, I haven't. I don't want to intrude on your meal."

"We've eaten. Come on through. We just had salads and cold meats. I'll grab you a plate of that and you can eat. But you're in casual clothes." Titus worked away preparing a meal for Aidan, knowing that Rachel would have told him to do that.

"I am. I'm off duty this weekend. I just stopped by hoping to find Taran and Thomas. I'm here as a friend, Titus, not an officer." Aidan took his plate of food with a word of thanks.

"You're welcome. Taran did say that we were all threatened." Titus poured two mugs of coffee, setting them on the table before he sat.

"You were. And we have no idea who or why. Not yet." Aidan looked around as he heard a faint sound. "Taran?"

"Aidan? I thought that you were working this weekend." Taran refused to enter the kitchen, Thomas standing behind her with a frown on his face.

"I'm not, Taran. And I'm not here as a detective. I'm here as a friend. You need that." Aidan grinned at her. "And what fun thing are you getting up to this weekend?"

Taran stared at him, not sure that she had heard him correctly.

"What are we up to? I have no idea. I need to go home, that's what I'm up to." Taran was holding her ground on that. She felt that she was putting others at risk by not being in her own home, even though the motel that she was registered at was safe and there was a patrol officer parked in front of her door overnight.

"We know that, Taran. We're releasing you on Monday. Until then, you're still sort of in our custody. Don and his men are working with us to make sure that you are safe." Aidan shared a look with Thomas.

"I know that. This is taking so much from everyone. And it shouldn't. I want it over and over yesterday." Taran felt Thomas' arms around her. She could hear soft comments from their parents as they stood just out of sight of the kitchen.

—

"It always does, Taran. It's what we work with all the time. Now, what can we do for you two?"

Taran shrugged, feeling Thomas' muffled laughter shaking his body.

"Thomas? This isn't funny." Her voice held tears. She was wearing down and discouraged, even though she tried her best to pray and trust. It was difficult at times to do that. She knew that God heard her prayers. It was in His timing, she had to acknowledge. She just wished that He would hurry up and end this adventure that she seemed to be on that she didn't want to be on.

"I know that it's not, darlin'. It's just that you and Aidan seem to be in a standoff about what we're up to this weekend. And we will do something fun. I promise you that." Thomas shook his head at Titus, knowing that Titus would be there with them and putting himself at risk for his brother's lady.

—

Chapter 18

Saturday found Taran up and ready to face the day. She had moved back home the night before, not letting anyone talk her out of it. She was afraid, she had to admit to herself, but determined to continue living. Taran was expecting Thomas shortly. He had given her no choice about the day, simply stating that she would spend the day with him. A twinkle in his eyes had had her frowning at him.

Walking through her home, Taran knew that she would sell it and move. She just wasn't sure if she would stay in that town. It had become difficult for her to do that, she had to acknowledge to herself. The text message the day before had shaken her to her core. To threaten her was one thing. To threaten her family changed the dynamics of what she was facing. Taran had spent the night in prayer, begging God to take the adventure away from her, begging Him to protect her family and friends, and then just waiting in silence for Him to speak. She had peace that morning but she knew that it might not last.

Thomas reached for her hand a while later, leading her to his truck and tucking her inside. He too had spent the night in prayer, searching for God's leading in all this. He knew that Taran was not safe, not yet anyway. He had spoken at length with Aidan that morning, just trying to get a sense of where the investigation stood. Aidan could not tell him much more than he already had. That frustrated both of them.

Taran watched around her, feeling eyes on her. She shuddered in fear for a moment before she turned her eyes to the bright blue sky. She was determined to enjoy that day, no matter how much it took from her. Paul and Payten were meeting them somewhere. Thomas hadn't told her where yet. She frowned as she saw him heading for the highway.

"Where are we heading, Thomas?"

"We're heading for Elmton. I haven't been there in a few months. I thought that a change of scenery would do both of us good." Thomas grinned at her before his eyes caught the truck following them in his mirrors. "Paul's behind us."

"That sounds like fun. I like your team members. And Payten is just too sweet. What are the rest up to?" Taran smiled brightly, her spirits lightening for the moment as the town disappeared in the rearview mirror.

"I have no idea. Some of them were heading away for the weekend. The others just hang around, do stuff at their homes, and destress until we meet up again at work on Monday." Thomas watched carefully for anyone around them. He couldn't see anyone but he knew that they were being followed. He prayed that God would defend them that day.

Noon found the two couples heading for a local diner, their faces still covered in smiles. Taran had relaxed at last, knowing that she was free for the moment of danger. Or was she? Taran wasn't quite sure about that.

Andrew McBeth, the Elmton police chief, looked up from his meal, his wife, Phoebe, sitting across from him. Toryn had been in touch, knowing that Thomas had planned to be in Andrew's town that day. He just had not expected to find Thomas in his aunt's diner.

Thomas looked around and then nodded at Andrew. He would call him later, just to touch base with him. Taran was watching him closely before her eyes met Andrew's. She frowned at him before she nodded. She knew who he was.

"Thomas? What are we to do?" Taran hated to ask and spoil their day but she felt that she had no choice.

"What are we to do?" Thomas shared a look with Paul. "For now, we enjoy our meal and then we explore some more of the town. I don't want to be late heading home."

Paul nodded, knowing that he had to leave soon. He and Payten had a commitment in Oak City that evening that they had to be at. He was not willing to miss it but would if Thomas felt that he needed him to stay.

Driving home in the late afternoon, Thomas was content for the moment. He reached for Taran's hand for a moment, his grasp tightening on hers as he felt hers returning the grasp. His eyes were on the move constantly, searching for someone who meant them harm. So far, they had been safe but he knew that could change in a moment.

—

Taran's head went back on the headrest on fthe seat. Her eyes closed as she dozed off. Today had been a wonderful day, her thoughts told her before she slept. She didn't see the truck that had approached them from behind.

Thomas' attention was on the road ahead of him. They were within a few miles of Oak City when the truck behind him made its move. It sped around him and pulled in front of him, slowing down and causing him to slow. Thomas frowned and then hit the brakes before he was turning his wheel. His foot hit the accelerator as his truck jumped ahead. Taran gave a small scream as she was jolted awake at Thomas' moves.

Thomas sped past the truck and back into his proper lane. His foot kept steady on the gas pedal as he headed for town. He could see the truck coming up behind him. Thomas searched for another way to escape, knowing that he was close to town. His foot pressed harder on the gas pedal, his phone tossed to Taran.

"Call it in, Taran. We need support and now. I'm not sure that I can escape the truck behind me." Thomas slowed and took a turn, knowing that he was placing them into danger but knowing that he didn't have much choice. His move was quick enough that the truck following him sped past.

His eyes searching, Thomas suddenly slammed on the brakes. The move brought a scream from Taran who stared at him in horror.

"Thomas? What are you doing?" Taran's hands clung to whatever she could find to brace herself.

"I'm hiding us until help arrives. That truck will be here in no time." Thomas spun the wheel and headed into a driveway. He knew the owners well as they were a family friend. He would hide there until help arrived.

His truck tucked away in the drive shed, Thomas reached for Taran's hand and pulled her from the front seat. He ran with her towards the house, knowing where to find a key. Unlocking the door, he shoved her inside and then locked the door behind them.

"Thomas? What is going on? Where are we?" Taran watched from the safety of the mudroom as Thomas walked through the house.

The homeowners were not home. He knew that they were away on holidays. His phone out, he sent the owner a text message, receiving a quick reply. He gave a grim smile. The retired officer stated that Thomas was welcome there even in danger.

Thomas returned to the mudroom, his eyes on Taran. He could see the fear in her eyes and knew that she was trying hard to hide it from him. He just reached to wrap her in his arms.

"This is a friend's place. It has good security. He was on a federal task force as an officer and needed to be safe. He's okay with us being here." Thomas moved away from her, hearing the sounds of a truck. "They're searching all the properties."

"They'll find us, won't they?" Taran was frozen in place with fear. She just knew that they would disappear. *God, where are You? Are You here? Did You protect us just now?*

Chapter 19

Thomas paced the kitchen and into the mudroom. Taran had simply refused to leave that room. He knew that she was terrified. He was afraid as well. His phone chiming caught at his attention.

"Thomas? Where are you?" Don's voice echoed across the airwaves. "Toryn called me to tell me that you were in danger."

"We are, Don. I'm hiding right now. I'm not sure when it will be safe to leave." Thomas turned to face Taran, seeing the fear now evident on her face. "I took the first road out of town." He didn't have to say much more. Don would figure it out.

"I see. I know where you are. What happened?" Don turned to Mark who was standing nearby. He simply pointed to the door, Mark nodding as he headed that way.

"Someone tried to stop me on the highway coming into town. Paul and Payten had left earlier as they had that commitment. Taran called it in but the truck followed us so the officers not likely found them."

"Were you able to catch a plate number?" Don started his truck, heading away from his home. Mark's eyes were on the move, not seeing anyone following them.

"I was. I sent it on to the department. They're actively looking for it." Thomas reached for Taran, drawing her to him. "The truck was in and out here.

They're searching the properties along this road. It's only a matter of time until they come back. I don't know that we'll have time to get back on the road and into town before they're back."

Taran was shaking with fear. Not even Thomas' arms around her could ease her fear. She tried to pray but just didn't think that God was listening to her.

Thomas tucked his phone away, moving Taran from the mud room to the kitchen. He prepared coffee for them, setting her mug on the table. She sat, not comfortable there. She was deeply afraid, knowing how close it had been.

"Thomas? We can't stay here. What are we to do?" Taran's face showed her fear. She just could not hide it any more.

"We can for now. Don has figured out where we are. He'll be here and bring reinforcements with him. We just need to stay here for now." Thomas set his own mug of coffee on the table before he tidied up the area. "Drink that. You're shaking and something hot may help." He grinned at her snort. "No?"

"I don't think so. Just having this over will help. How close are we to that?" Taran prayed that it would be over that day. Only, she didn't think that her prayers would be heard.

"I have no idea, Taran. Aidan hasn't said. If it was close to being over, he would have told us." Thomas smiled in sympathy as her face crumpled for a moment before she controlled her tears. "It's okay to cry, darlin'. I'll just hold you until you're done if that's what you need."

"I don't cry, did you know that? I seem to be doing that too much lately." She sighed, knowing that she had just become vulnerable in front of him. That was something that she never did, not even in front of her parents. "I just worry about our families and your team mates."

"My team mates know what to watch out for. They'll take the precautions that they need to. And they'll make sure that our families are as safe as they can be." Thomas reached for her hand, his head bowing as he prayed for them. He prayed all the verses of protection and safety that he could think of. He could feel Taran relaxing as he did so.

Taran raised her head as she heard a vehicle. Fear shot through her and she ran for the mudroom, hiding in there once more. Thomas nodded, heading for a window. He stood to one side, watching closely as the truck that had tailed him stopped and two men exited. Thomas knew that his truck wasn't visible and that the drive shed door was locked as were the house doors. He didn't think that the tire tracks would show on the gravel driveway.

The men approached the house, trying the doors and then trying to open the windows. They were unsuccessful. Thomas could hear them arguing, a frown on his face as he recognized one of the voices. This was not good, he decided. That was a probation officer out there. How deep did this go?

Thomas walked quietly back towards Taran, a finger on his lips to stop her questions. He stood beside her, an arm holding her close to his side. She shook for a moment with the fear wafting through her before she laid her head against his shoulder. Thomas made her feel safe in a way that not even her parents did.

Hearing another vehicle, Thomas hesitated before he moved to the window once more, Taran's hand still in his. He tucked her to the side as he watched the activity outside. Don and Mark had arrived, confronting the two men who had chased them. Thomas could see the agitation of the two men and Don and Mark standing their ground. The men finally left, a cloud of dust sifting back to the ground. Mark walked to the road, watching carefully to make sure that they left. He knew that Caleb and Joshua were at the corner of the road and would follow the truck.

Don waited for a time, leaving Mark to walk the property before he headed for the back door. Thomas opened the door to Mark who slipped in quietly.

"Mark?" Thomas' voice had the question that both he and Taran wanted to ask.

"They're gone. Caleb and Joshua are tailing them. Paul was in touch. He's working on finding out what he can on them. The plate number worked well."

"I know. One of them is a probation officer." Thomas heard Taran's quickly indrawn breath. "Taran?"

"George has a nephew who is a probation officer. Was that him?" Taran drew in a deep breath. "Is that the connection that we've been looking for?"

"We'll look into it, Taran. For now, we'll get you home. You do want to go home?" Mark watched her carefully, seeing how she moved closer to Thomas.

"I do but is it safe to do that?" Taran felt Thomas pulling her towards the door. She shook off his hand to return to the kitchen and clean up their coffee mugs.

Mark watched her carefully and saw how tense that Taran was. He shared a look with Thomas who merely nodded. Mark could do nothing more than pray for the couple.

Chapter 20

Walking around her home that night, Taran searched for anything that was out of the ordinary. She didn't think that there was but she just wasn't sure. Having suspected that it was George's nephew who had tried to kidnap them that day had rattled her. She wondered if Junior as he was known by had had anything to do with George's death. Taran was afraid, she had to admit. Her mother had called her just as she had arrived home, just to ask how her day had been. Taran had not told her what had happened on the way home. She knew that she needed to tell them but was hesitant to.

Rachel had turned to Tam, walking into his hug. She was afraid for her daughter but didn't know how to protect her. Tam felt the same. He worried about his daughter, his worry growing every day. He had had a long talk with Thomas who had been upfront with him about the danger that Taran was in.

Thomas thoughtfully set his phone to one side, reaching to plug it into a charger. Today had not ended as he wanted it to, that was a given, he decided. Taran had been threatened once more and he could not have prevented it. He had spoken with Aidan when he arrived home. Aidan had not been surprised that someone had tried to abduct them again. He just had not been prepared to hear that George's nephew was a probation officer. This changed things, did he know, he had asked Thomas. Thomas had laughed at him and acknowledged that he had been surprised as well.

———

Then, he asked Aidan how much the family members of George and the staff at the pharmacy had been looked into. Aidan had not replied, knowing that was something that should have been done and obviously had not. Another detective had been assigned to George's murder.

Toryn had set aside his own phone after speaking with Aidan. He could tell Aidan to take the weekend off but he just sometimes couldn't do that. He was disturbed by Aidan's call. Toryn knew who the detective was. He reached for his phone again, reaching out to Emma. She had agreed to investigate the detective. She had not liked what he had told her.

Monday found Taran walking towards her pharmacy building. She was later than she had wanted to arrive but the patrol officer had insisted on inspecting her home and then her vehicle. She could see the officer making his rounds of the building and then waiting for her to unlock the door and turn off the security system. Taran had changed the locks and the security system as soon as she had taken over the pharmacy. Toryn had simply insisted on that for her. She had looked at him and then nodded.

Reaching to hang up her jacket, Taran paused. Something was off in the office. She turned and almost ran for the door, flagging down the officer as he was walking back to his vehicle. He returned.

"Bob? Something is off in the office. I don't know what. Can you take a better look?" Taran stood in the hallway, watching as Bob walked through her office, searching for whatever it was that had disturbed

Taran. He paused at the desk, his eyes on the package sitting there.

"Taran? This package? When did it come?" Bob beckoned her into the room.

"That package? I don't know. It wasn't here Friday when I locked up. I was away on Saturday. It must have come then. Joe would know." Taran reached for her phone, her hand stopping as Bob shook his head. "Bob?"

"Let us reach out to him, Taran. For now, I need to bring in a tech to look at this. Can you work around us?" Bob waited patiently for her to think through what that would mean.

"I can. On Monday morning, there is only myself and one other staff for the first hour. The pharmacy tech comes in at ten o'clock. We'll manage." Taran walked away, heading for the pharmacist counter and reaching for the faxes that had come in since Saturday. She didn't like this, not one bit. She just knew that she was going to have to give up her dream and she was not prepared to do that.

Aidan waited outside for Bob to approach him. He had taken Bob's short call and then made his way to the pharmacy. He didn't know what was in the package but Bob's call had alarmed him. This was beginning to pick up for Taran and that meant it was becoming more dangerous for her.

"Bob? What was in the package?" Aidan asked the question, not sure what the response would be.

"I don't know as yet. The two techs are working on it. They know that you're here and will ask for you to come in when they're ready. Taran is shaken by this." Bob knew that she wouldn't say much. She hadn't and he had been the one who had been working with her in the mornings.

"No, she won't. She doesn't need this. It's difficult enough taking on a new business without facing danger." Bob nodded towards the back door. "They're looking for you, Aidan."

"Aidan?" Belle, the tech, pointed to the office. "This is strange. It seems to be a threat but it is not one that we have ever seen." She was puzzled at what they had found.

Aidan gave her a look before heading into the office. The other tech stood back, a puzzled look on his face as well.

"Dave? What is it?" Aidan didn't wait for a response. Instead, he approached the desk and stopped. He stared down into the box, a puzzled look on his own face. "This is what was in it?"

"It is. A stuffed bear. And a dead red rose. We need to get this back to the lab and look it over better. My gut tells me that something else is in there."

Aidan nodded, watching as the package was placed in evidence bags. He had taken the photos that he needed to for himself. He turned to walk to the door that led to the store, his eyes on Taran as she worked away, a smile on her face as she greeted her customers. He felt that the store was busier than it had been. Bob stood beside him.

"The store is busy." Aidan's comment filled the silence that had grown between the two men.

"It has gotten busier since Taran took over. George was making a go of it, but something changed when Taran took over. I don't understand it." Bob walked away, heading back for the streets and his patrol.

Taran looked up at that point, her eyes meeting Aidan. She did not like it that he was there, but she knew that he would have been called in, given that it was her. She drew in a deep breath, taking a break. The pharmacy technician looked up as Taran spoke to her and then walked away.

"Aidan? I don't like the look on your face." She came to a halt beside him.

Aidan pointed to her office, waiting for her to sit at her desk. She stared at the desktop, knowing that danger had sat there not too long ago.

"I don't like it either, Taran. That package? It contained a stuffed bear and a dead red rose. It was a threat, directed at you. But we think that there was something else in there. The techs will look at it in more detail in the lab. But for now? They had not only challenged and treated you at your home. They are reaching out to your business. How do we keep you safe?" Aidan's words were biting, not directed at Taran but at the circumstances that were occurring.

"Who is doing this, Aidan? I'm looking at having to hire already. We were never this busy with George. It doesn't make a lot of sense." Taran rose once more, heading for the pharmacy counter. She had work to do. A threat to her wasn't stopping the work that was needing to be done.

Chapter 21

Thomas knew without being told that Taran had not had a good day. He could tell by her posture. She was trying to hide it from him, he knew, in order not to worry him. It didn't work. He simply moved into her space and wrapped her into a hug. Thomas felt her clinging to him, silent sobs shaking her body.

"What happened, darlin'? Something did." He waited for her to speak. He had been followed closely himself that day and he had just let them. He wanted it over and over that day. But that wasn't likely to happen.

"I had a package on my desk at the store today. Aidan took it away. It scared me, Thomas. I want this over and it doesn't seem to be happening. Who is doing this to us? It's not just me. They've been watching us. Who sends a lady a dead red rose? Is that a threat directed at you?"

"A dead red rose? What else?" Thomas again waited for her to gather her thoughts and then tell him.

"A stuffed bear. Aidan seemed to think that something else was there. He hasn't told me yet." Taran leaned against Thomas, feeling safe but knowing that she wasn't nor was he.

"He will when he can. Now, what can I do for you?" Thomas waited patiently once more for her to decide what she wanted to do.

"I don't know, Thomas. How do we do this? They are following you, they said. They're upping their threats towards me. What do we do? We need to stop seeing one another."

"It won't make any difference. They have seen us together and they'll still go after one of us to get to the other. We still have not figured out why." Thomas turned her back to her home, shutting the door after him. He was worried as was his team. They had been working it but had made no progress. That puzzled and worried them all.

"Has your team found out anything?" Taran walked towards her office, sitting at her desk. "How do we search?"

"We don't, Taran. We're trying to work it but there is something missing. We need to start working on who we know. Our friends. Our families. Those that we work with."

"Here." She handed him a piece of paper that contained everyone who she could think of.

"You've been busy. So have I." He pulled out a sheet of paper from his pocket. "Here. Let's see who we know in common. I think that is what we'll find. We know people in common. We just have to figure out who."

"Here. You work on it. I have my list on the computer. Work on putting yours on it and then we can sort it." Taran had an eye on the clock and knew that it was time for them to eat. She headed for the kitchen, finding something for them to eat. She headed back for the office, a tray in her hands.

Thomas looked up as she entered. He had taken a call from Emma, her words sending him pen flying across the paper. She had found evidence that they needed to talk about but first they would eat.

Setting aside his phone, Thomas rose and went to sit beside Taran. He wasn't content just to hold her hand as he asked the blessing on their meal. He wrapped her with his arm, drawing her close to him.

"Thomas? Who were you speaking with?"

"Emma. She's sent some information. I need to reach out to the others." He looked around as he heard the doorbell. "Were you expecting anyone?"

"No." Taran stopped as she went to rise.

Thomas was on his feet, heading for the door. He stepped backwards as his team and Payten appeared.

"You're here?"

Don nodded, heading past Thomas to where he could see Taran.

"Emma called me. She said that she was calling you but that we needed to meet."

"We do. We're just grabbing a meal. I have some information on the computer. Go ahead." Thomas waited as Paul hesitated beside him. "Paul?"

"Just how are you doing, Thomas? It's tough when our ladies are in trouble and we can't solve it. What can I do for you?"

"It is hard, Paul. I never appreciated how bad it was with you and Payten. I do now. I know that God is in control. I can feel His presence. So can Taran. It doesn't make it easier."

"No, it doesn't. Now, what can we do to solve this and quickly?" Paul gave a quick grin.

Thomas listened to Taran and Payten talking and then saw them rise and move to the living room. He watched as their heads bowed and they prayed. He was glad for this. Taran needed that support from a lady who had gone through this type of event. Thomas knew a number of other ladies that he could put her in touch with and would.

Joshua looked around, catching Thomas' eye. He moved towards his friend.

"Joshua? What did you find?" Thomas sat, taking the paper that Joshua was shoving at him.

"This. Do you know how many people you two know in common? This makes it hard."

"It does and it doesn't. I sent the list on to Emma and she said that she had Jace working on it. They'll find out what we need to know before we do. Anyone up for a challenge?"

The men laughed before they once more dug into what they were looking at. They took turns at the computer before Don was out of the house and back with his laptop. That did help to some degree.

Taran listened to them, adding her voice as she needed to. Payten in turn watched Taran, finally drawing her away once more.

117

“I know these guys. They’ll need to eat. What do you have that we can serve them?” Payten grinned as Taran shook her head.

“I know. I have lots of bread and sandwich fillings. We can make sandwiches.” Taran was on the move, heading for her freezer. “And I have some squares and cookies that I made. I was bored the other night and couldn’t sleep. I ended up baking instead.”

Chapter 22

On the Friday of that week, Thomas and Mark walked towards Ben's diner. They had finished work for the week and just needed to relax. Thomas glanced at his watch. Taran would not be finished work as yet. It was the day that she worked somewhat later than the others. He had spoken with her earlier and they had agreed to meet on the Saturday to do something fun.

The sound of running feet startled the two men. Thomas began to swing around but didn't make it all the way around. He was down on the pavement before he could react. Mark struggled with his attacker, face down on the ground. Thomas felt his arms wrangled behind him, unable to react before he felt handcuffs clicking around his wrists. Hauling to his feet, he was shoved forward, his feet tangling with one another as he tried to regain his balance.

Mark lay on the pavement, unmoving. The blow that he had taken to the back of his head had left him motionless. He didn't hear the yells of the pedestrians or the running footsteps that approached him. He also didn't hear the sirens of the emergency personnel as they responded.

Ben stood nearby, having heard the commotion and appearing to see what had happened. He drew in a deep breath as he recognized Mark. His eyes searched the crowds, stopping as he saw an undercover officer watching from a nearby building. He walked that way, stopping beside the young officer.

"Brenn? Did you see what happened?" Ben knew that Brenn would be looking for a patrol officer to speak with.

"They were taken down, Ben. Thomas was hustled away. I couldn't step in. There just wasn't time." Brenn was upset that he had been unable to help Thomas.

"I didn't think that you could. They'll be around to speak with you." Ben looked around, seeing Aidan approaching him. "Aidan's here."

"I know." Brenn disappeared, not wanting to speak with Aidan at that time.

"Ben? What happened here? Did you see it?" Aidan frowned as he saw the man who disappeared. He thought he knew him but he wasn't positive on it.

"I didn't see it happen. I just heard all the yelling. That's Mark, isn't it?" Ben didn't let on that he had spoken with Brenn. Brenn would reach out as he needed to. He also knew that Brenn would be searching for Thomas.

"It is. Who was with him?" Aidan wasn't sure which of the team would have been.

"I don't know for sure." Ben walked away, heading back for the diner. He reached for his phone, turning it over before he called Don.

"Don? It's Ben. Who was with Mark this afternoon?" Ben could hear the sounds of water running into a sink and knew that he had caught Don preparing his supper. The sounds of the water stopped.

"Thomas was. They were heading for your place for a meal. Why?" Don reached to turn off the stove, setting the pot of potatoes that weren't quite cooked into the sink and then reaching to pull the meat from the oven.

"Mark is hurt. He was taken down near the diner. Thomas is nowhere in sight. Someone on the street told me that Thomas was taken away." Ben could hear Don's footsteps as he almost ran across his wooden flooring heading for the outside door.

"Where are you?" Don's truck headed for the street and towards the diner.

"At the diner. Aidan is here."

"How bad was Mark hurt?" Don slowed as he approached the area, finding a place to park. His feet took him rapidly towards the scene of activity.

"I don't know. He wasn't responding when I saw him. They may have moved off with him by now."

Aidan turned from where he stood near the scene, taking notes. Don paused beside him, waiting for him to turn and speak with him.

"Don? Who called you?" Aidan had not expected to see Don at the scene.

"Ben. He let me know that Mark was injured. And that Thomas is nowhere around."

"Thomas? He was with Mark?" Aidan's pen stopped as he stared at Don.

"He was. They had headed here for a meal. Thomas said that Taran was working late tonight, until six I think. They weren't planning on seeing each other tonight."

"Then, Thomas is missing." Aidan walked away, heading for a patrol officer. They now needed to start a search. Only Aidan didn't think that they would find Thomas or find him soon.

Don reached for his keys, heading back for his truck. He knew that Aidan would reach out to Thomas' family. He needed to head for Taran. He glanced at his watch, trying to determine where she might be.

Taran stepped back from her garage door, staring at the truck that pulled into her driveway. She frowned. It was Don who had arrived. Sudden fear and apprehension flowed through her. *Lord, please let Thomas be okay. I fear for him. Don is not here for my health, not this time.*

"Don? What happened? It's Thomas, isn't it?" Taran's words ran together in her fear.

"It is. Inside, Taran. I need to speak with you." Don didn't give her any option. His hand reached for her arm, tugging her towards the house. He shut the door and locked it after them.

"Don? What is the meaning of this?" Taran spun and stared at him.

"Taran, have you heard from Thomas this afternoon?" Don watched her closely, seeing her frown at his question.

"No, I haven't. We were to talk later tonight. What happened to him?" Taran began to pray for her guy, knowing that Don would not be here or asking the questions that he was unless something had happened.

"He's disappeared, Taran. He and Mark were heading for Ben's when they were attacked. Mark is unconscious and on his way to the hospital. Thomas has disappeared."

Taran's face coloured with horror as she heard Don's words. She began to shake violently. This was what she had feared and prayed would never happen. Only, it had. Taran had to trust that God was in control and that He was with Thomas, wherever Thomas was. She just didn't expect it to happen.

"Thomas? Please, Lord, not that." Taran fought her tears.

Don watched with compassion before his hand was on her arm, forcing her to sit. He reached to plug in the kettle, intent on making her a cup of tea that he would sweeten even though he was aware that she would fight him on that. Don then reached for his phone, calling her parents and then calling Daci, who simply asked what she could do and that she was on her way.

Chapter 23

Daci watched her friend closely, knowing that she would speak when she was ready to. She just didn't know how to approach her or what to say to her. She simply walked up to her, wrapped her in a hug, and began to pray for her.

Daci's prayer shook Taran's composure and she began to weep. She didn't know where Thomas was. She feared for his life. Daci turned her friend to the living room, shoving her down on the couch and reaching for her hands, continuing to pray for her. She knew that there were patrol officers outside, sent by Aidan. Her parents were on their way, coming back from Elmton. Don had left, simply stating that he was heading for the hospital.

Don paced the waiting room, his eyes raising to the doors leading to the Emergency Room examination rooms. He didn't know how seriously hurt that Mark was. The other team members paced as well. He turned to see Payten sitting with Rose and Thaddeus. Titus was away for the weekend, not easily reached by phone. They had insisted on being there for Mark, knowing that his own family was many miles away.

Turning as he heard his name called, Don walked towards the nurse who pointed him towards one of the rooms. He stood in the doorway, hearing Mark's voice answering questions fired at him by Aidan. Don walked to stand nearby, catching Mark's eye.

Aidan studied Don and then turned back to Mark.

"You didn't see anything?" Aidan knew that Mark not likely had.

"Not a thing. We were talking with one another. The next thing that I knew, I'm waking up here. Where's Thomas?" Mark's eyes shifted between Don and Aidan before his head went back on the pillow and his eyes closed. "He's disappeared?"

"He has. We don't have much information as yet. Officers are searching for him and asking around that area. So far, we haven't had any word on where he is." Aidan walked away at last, not happy that Mark could not give him much information.

Don watched Aidan leave before turning back to Mark.

"Mark? You're okay to leave?"

"I am. Where are we meeting?" Mark swung his legs off the stretcher, waiting for the dizziness to ease.

"Taran's. Daci is with her right now as are her parents. Thomas' family is heading that way." Don pointed at the door. "You have your discharge paperwork?"

"I do. Let's go." Mark wobbled for a moment as his feet hit the floor before he stiffened his knees. He headed for the door, Don following him.

Toryn watched as the two men walked away and then turned to walk away himself. He saw that Don's group had left the waiting room. He nodded. They would be all heading for Taran. She needed their support. His phone chiming had him pausing to read the message. Nodding, Toryn headed for Ben's.

Brenn had been in touch with Don and wanted to speak with him.

Taran turned as she heard more footsteps entering her house. She paled at the number of people there before she stiffened her spine and moved to greet them. She stopped in front of Mark, studying his face before he swept her into a hug and prayed for her. Taran stepped back, a frown on her face.

"Mark? Should you be here? Weren't you hurt?" Taran watched his face closely, seeing the pain from his headache. "Have you taken anything for your headache?"

"I have, thank you, Taran. Now, where are we meeting?" He grinned at her before his arm was around her shoulders, turning her towards her office. "Your office?"

"I think so. I don't work tomorrow, thank goodness." Taran slipped to a seat, fatigue suddenly hitting her hard.

"That's good. We want to keep you safe, Taran. Thomas may well have been taken to draw you out. You've been well protected over the last few weeks. That is frustrating them. Thomas would rather it be him who is taken rather than one of your parents." Mark watched with compassion as Taran took in his words.

"They would do that, wouldn't they?" Taran bit at her lip, uncertainty on her face. "How do we keep them safe?"

Tam sat beside his daughter, his arm around her. She turned to him, seeing his worry for her on his face.

"Dad?"

"We'll be okay, Taran. Mark is right. They may have gone after us to get to you, but they will use Thomas instead. Everyone can see that he cares about you. A boyfriend is likely better to use as a bargaining chip or threat. They could use Mom or me but that doesn't make a lot of sense." Tam shared a look with Mark who was nodding.

"I get that, Dad. I just don't know why. What do they want from me?" Taran turned as Thaddeus spoke up.

"Your pharmacy. They can use it for illegal drugs at the very least." Thaddeus had been researching and investigating on his own. He had also talked with both Richard and Abe.

"I know that. We don't keep a large stock of what they would want for illicit sales of drugs." Taran was confused. "I just don't see that."

"There has to be a connection between George's death and the pharmacy. Do you have all the paperwork that was there?" Joshua spoke up, a thought crossing his mind.

"I have it here. I had wanted to go over it but haven't taken the time. If it helps solve this and brings Thomas home, you're welcome to go through it." Taran was on her feet, heading for a filing cabinet, Joshua following. "Here. Use the dining room table to sort it out."

Taran walked the house as she listened to the various conversations. She yawned, suddenly tired but not willing to sleep yet. The men had settled into the office and dining room. She looked around for Daci and the two moms, finding them in the sunroom. She sank down beside Daci, grateful for their support.

Rachel watched her daughter carefully, seeing the strain on her face. She prayed for her, petitioning God to protect and defend her and to bring Thomas back home.

Chapter 24

Thomas shook his head as he picked himself up from the rough dirt floor that he had landed on. He felt the debris and stones that bit into his hands and knees. He looked around, frustrated that he was a captive. How did he manage to get away? And who had done this?

Locked into a shed, Thomas searched for a way to escape. He had no idea where he had been taken. A blindfold had been slapped roughly across his eyes after he had been shoved into a vehicle. The handcuffs had bitten into his wrists as he twisted his wrists, trying to escape. Thomas rubbed at his wrists. They were scraped, but that was the least of his concerns. How was Taran? Had she been kidnapped as well?

Not finding a way out, Thomas leaned against a wall, feeling the roughness of the wood through his cotton shirt. He shivered slightly in the dampness of the room. How was he to escape?

Night fell and then morning came. Thomas still stood leaning against the wall. He wasn't sure what he was waiting for but God had spoken to him overnight, assuring him that he would be free that day.

A scraping at the back wall of the shed had Thomas moving that way. He listened carefully, hope rising within him as he recognized the voice. Brenn had found him. Brenn was a friend from the streets, Thomas knew, but Thomas didn't realize that Brenn was also an officer.

Thomas began to push at the board that was moving, shifting it enough for him to wiggle through and out. The two men shoved the board back into place before Brenn pointed to their left. They moved out rapidly, almost on a run, as they could hear the shouts of frustration coming from the direction of the shed.

Sliding to a halt at last, Thomas leaned against a rundown brick building. A frown covered his face for a moment. He was still in town? He hadn't realized that he had not been taken out of his town.

"Brenn? How did you find me?" Thomas kept his voice low.

"It wasn't too hard. I recognized the men, knew where they were staying, and just searched. I knew that they had more than one hiding place. After searching all night, I found you this morning. Now, off with you. Your truck is still where you left it. I heard that no one had a key for it other than you and Titus." Brenn pointed towards where the diner was.

"And he is out of town. Thanks, Brenn." Thomas was off with rapid strides, knowing that Brenn wanted no thanks other than what he had been given. In his truck, he hesitated for a moment, not sure where to head. His phone needed to be charged and he couldn't call anyone.

Squinting at the sky and noting that dawn was just breaking, Thomas headed for his home. He felt grubby and needed to clean up. Showered, shaved, and in clean clothes, he reached for his mug of coffee, sipping at it before he set it aside. He reached instead for his Bible, needing to spend time with his Lord.

An hour later, Thomas locked his front door, heading for his truck. His feet slowed as he recognized the man waiting there.

"Richard? You're here?" Thomas stopped in front of him.

"I am. Don called us in last night. Taran was positive that you were home this morning. We had to physically restrain her from leaving her home. There are a number of us gathering there to investigate. Come on, Thomas. Let's get you to your lady. And Aidan is there." Richard didn't ask what had happened. He knew better.

"Thanks, Richard. I've been home for about an hour or so." Thomas watched the passing scenery, still trying to process what had happened.

Richard paused at Taran's driveway before he shoved the truck gears into park.

"I don't know what happened. You will tell us, Thomas, once you've spoken with Aidan. But I must say. Taran has been like a terrier with a rat. She just had not stopped all night. None of us could get her to. Now that you're here, she may collapse from fatigue and release of stress." Richard watched him carefully.

"I get that, Richard. I figured as much. It's just so strange, what happened." Thomas was out of the truck, heading for the front door.

Mark opened the door at his tap, standing in shock to see Thomas.

"Thomas? What? How?" Mark didn't seem able to put a single sentence together. He then pointed towards the sun room. "In there. She's by herself for now."

Thomas hesitated at the door, watching Taran as she sat huddled up on the loveseat, a blanket wrapped around her. His feet took him forward towards her.

Taran hesitated before she looked up. She thought that she could sense Thomas near her but that wasn't possible. He was still missing. Her eyes raised to find Thomas standing in front of her. On her feet, untangling herself from her blanket, she simply threw herself into his arms.

Thomas held the lady who he had admitted to himself in the overnight hours that he was in love with. He thought that she had feelings for him but that was something that they would discuss in the days to come. Right now, he was safe and with her.

Taran looked up at him, a puzzled look on her face.

"Thomas? You're here? What happened? Aidan said that you had disappeared and they didn't know where you were."

"I did. A friend found me and helped me to escape. I'm glad that I'm back with you. Did you sleep at all last night?" His smile was tender as he looked down at her.

"Not really. I spent it in prayer. Everyone here kept checking on me." Taran turned him towards the hallway. "They'll need to talk with you. Aidan was around but had to leave."

Tam looked around, surprise on his face before he touched Thaddeus on the shoulder and nodded behind him. Thaddeus turned, stared at Thomas, and then was on his feet. He wrapped his son in a hard hug before he let Rose have her turn. He then turned to Taran and found her wrapped in her father's arms. Tam shook his head at Thaddeus before he began to pray.

The others in the room had looked up and then risen to their feet. Their voices picked up the chain of prayer.

Thomas looked around at his friends and family. He had been defended by God and released from captivity. Now, he was determined to find the men who had abducted him and finally bring them to justice.

Chapter 25

Aidan turned from his office, on a search for Toryn. He couldn't find him in the building and then stood outside, a hand rubbing at his cheek. His fingers snapped as he decided on something and then ran for his car. Heading for the downtown area, Aidan parked near the diner. He didn't go into the building. Instead, Aidan headed for a nearby park, purchasing coffees and a sandwich. He sat, waiting patiently.

Brenn studied Aidan for a moment before he studied the area around them. He nodded. It was clear for him to approach him. Sitting beside him, he kept to the character that he had developed, that as someone down and out and hard on their luck.

Aidan simply handed over the sandwich and one of the coffee. It was a common ploy between the two of them.

"Brenn? What can you tell me?" He waited patiently as Brenn bit into the sandwich and then sipped at the coffee.

"Thomas is home. I found him about a mile from there. We watched the houses that we know that they have. We finally tracked one down early this morning. He was locked in a shed outside."

Nodding slightly, Aidan sipped at his own coffee.

"Thank you, Brenn. Let me have the address. We'll be looking into it. Was Thomas hurt?"

"Not that I could see. He did have scrapes on his wrists, likely from the handcuffs. I made sure that he found Taran." Brenn was on his feet, walking away and getting lost in the people that were mingling around.

Knocking at Taran's front door, Aidan waited for someone to answer. Tam was there, his eyes surprised at seeing him.

"Aidan? You're here? I don't know that anyone of us called you."

"No one did. I was told that Thomas is here." Aidan stepped inside, his eyes on Thomas. "Thomas? We need to talk and now."

"I know. I haven't said anything, Aidan. I was going to head into the department in a few minutes."

Sitting back in his chair as he read Thomas' statement, Aidan frowned.

"You don't have much of a statement."

"No, I don't. Not much happened. I don't know the men. I don't know where I was kept. Brenn released me and brought me home."

"I hear that he did. Let me run with this and see what I can find. I'll be reaching out to a friend of Richard's. The one who is a title searcher." Aidan was on his feet and leaving, Thomas staring after him before he wrapped an arm around Taran.

"How did Aidan get here?" Taran was not really surprised to see him.

"I don't know. Someone told him that I was free. He seemed to think that I would find you. Now, where do we stand in our investigation?" Thomas turned her back to the office, surprised to find that she was just refusing to move.

"I don't know, Thomas. We're missing something. I need to visualize it and can't." Taran looked up as he began to laugh.

"We'll head for the office building, Taran. Pack up everything we need. We have white boards there that we can use." Thomas hugged her before he was calling for Don, suggesting that they all move to the office building.

Don agreed. It was where that they needed to be. They were hampered somewhat without the programs that they could use and needed to use. Emma had been in touch, letting him know that someone was on their way to find him. Just where would he be?

Don approached him, assessing him. He nodded before he stood and watched him carefully.

"Thomas? We need to figure this out. They'll just keep going after you to get to Taran." Don watched Taran as she stood with her mother's arm around her, Daci close to her side.

"I know. They never asked for anything, Don. Just locked me in that shed. Brenn was the one who found me. He mentioned that they have a number of buildings that they searched around." Thomas found his team grouped around him. "We don't have anyone in next week, do we?"

"No, we don't. We were looking at doing training ourselves. This investigation will become our training. We'll get there. Now, how be we pack up and head for the office? The ladies want to work this with us. Abe and Emma are heading this way as are Richard and his team. We'll start working on what we can. I don't think it will be long before we find the ones responsible."

Caleb shared a look with Mark and then Joshua, Paul nodding as he had a good idea of what Caleb was going to say.

"I don't know that it's the pharmacy, Don. That seems too obvious. There has to be a connection between George and Taran other than that. Micah from Abe's team was in touch. Kataleen was asking for family information so that she could start a family tree on George and on both Taran and Thomas."

Taran had been listening. This had been the conclusion that she had arrived at overnight. She had spent time going through all the verses about God's protection and defense as well as those that expressed hope and peace. She had found the peace and hope in God that she needed.

"That's what I think, Caleb. It never made sense. George was upfront with me when we discussed my purchase of the pharmacy. Unless something happened outside of the hours that I worked, I didn't see anyone around who would have threatened him. It just seems strange that the pharmacy has gotten busier since I took it over."

Paul frowned at her, a thought running through his mind.

"What you just said, Taran? It's gotten busier?"

"It has, Paul. I just don't understand it." Taran was puzzled by that.

Packing up everything, the group sorted themselves out into vehicles. Thomas refused to let go of Taran, climbing into the back of his father's truck. His parents just exchanged glances, amused looks in their eyes. They could well remember the first glow of young love. They would not say anything but would instead pray for their children. Taran had wrapped herself around their heart strings, becoming a part of their family without really trying.

Chapter 26

Late that afternoon, Thomas rose and stretched, his hands reaching for the ceiling. He walked away from the others, seeking quietness to pray. He didn't know when he had last felt this fatigued and worn out. Part of it he knew was because Taran was in his life. Thomas wanted to protect her but just didn't know how to do that. He had had deep conversations with Paul and then with Richard and his team. They could tell him what they had felt but they could not fully understand how he was feeling.

Titus followed his brother, staying back as he saw him find a quiet corner. He too found a corner to pray for his older brother. He had no idea how to pray for what Thomas was going through. All he could do was claim the promises of God for both Thomas and Taran.

Don walked away at last, heading for his house. He knew that the ladies were in his house, raiding his food stores to make a meal. He paused as he watched them, his eyes resting the longest on Taran. He then turned for his office, his phone out as he pondered who to call. Don knew that he had to talk to someone. He looked around as he heard footsteps. Thomas approached the office, dropping into a chair across the desk from Don.

"Don? Did we find anything that will help? I think that we are but I'm too close to the situation." Thomas' eyes closed for a moment.

"We are, Thomas. We are. We've narrowed it down to a group here in town. We just need to continue to work towards finding what all we can. The problem is keeping you and Taran safe." Don watched Thomas closely, seeing the stress and strain that Thomas was feeling.

"I get that, Don. I just want this over. Taran needs to be free again." Thomas kept his eyes on his hands, not looking around as he heard footsteps.

Aidan stood for a moment watching Thomas before looking at Don. He shook his head as he headed to a seat beside Thomas. He waited patiently, knowing that Thomas was sorting through his thoughts.

Thomas looked around, surprised to see Aidan there. He had not heard him enter and that bothered him. His senses were down, he knew, fatigue causing that. Thomas needed to sleep but didn't want to, not until this was solved.

"Aidan? What do we do know? This is wearing both of us out. Taran needs to get her life back and she can't. Not while she's threatened. I don't think it has to do with George. Her pharmacy business has grown since she bought the business. Do you know why?" Thomas was thinking aloud, not sure what to say.

"I understand that, Thomas. We are working that way. I wish I could say that we know who it is. We don't. We know who owns the house where you were imprisoned. We just don't see the connection between that couple and all of this. I have spoken with the man. They have been out of town on an extended vacation. He was horrified to hear what happened. They have a house sitter watching the house for them. I have that name but have been unable to find him to speak with him."

"You won't find him, Aidan." Taran spoke from the doorway. "He'll be dead and buried somewhere." Taran walked into the room to stand beside Thomas, a hand resting on his shoulder. Thomas wrapped an arm around her to pull her closer to him.

"Is that what you think? Why?" Aidan was surprised at her words but when he thought through it, he knew that he shouldn't have been.

Taran shrugged, not sure why she felt that way.

"It just seems strange. Why would they take Thomas and not ask anything of him? Who were they threatening by doing that? It can't be me. Was it Don?"

Don shot a look at her before he shared a look with Thomas, who was nodding. Taran had just confirmed his thoughts.

"I think that you are right, darlin'." His term of endearment had Taran frowning at him. He didn't realize that he was doing that. "It just didn't make sense if they were trying to get to you. They should have just taken you, not me. Whoever it is after you is keeping a very close eye on you. That worries me." Thomas shared a look with Don, who nodded. "This? Taking me this way without demanding anything? It's like it was a threat directed at someone. And that someone is not you. We always felt that something was left over from Paul's adventure."

______

"That we did, Thomas. We couldn't figure out what though." Don sat back, deep in thought.

"You did? And you didn't tell me?" Taran was growing angry, not at the man holding her or his friends. It was anger at the situation. She sighed to herself. She needed to ask forgiveness from the Lord and give Him her anger. Only, she didn't want to.

Thomas watched the emotions crossing her face, recognizing the anger and then the longing for all this to be over. He wanted to date Taran, not wanting her to walk away from him ever.

Don watched the couple, deciding that they had indeed become a couple whether they realized it or not. He caught the look in Thomas' eye and knew that he had indeed found his lady. He prayed for healing for the paramedic on his team. There would need to be not just physical healing, he knew. Don prayed for a touch of the Master's garment on both Thomas and Taran.

"Taran, it will be over. We're getting close to where we need to be. Emma is funnelling information to us and to Aidan. She said that she and Abe would likely make a trip here in the next couple of days. Another friend is working on a suspect profile. It's what Darci does."

Taran sighed, seeing dollar signs in front of her eyes.

"I am going to owe so many people so much." She looked between the two men as they laughed. "I will. I just know that I will." Her voice was despondent.

"Emma never charges friends for what she does. Nor does Darci. They both went through some pretty horrible things with their husbands. Darci almost died at the hands of a rogue police chief. It didn't matter that her fiancé at the time and now husband is an ETF lieutenant."

"That's horrible. But God was there, wasn't He? He is here, protecting and defending us. I just wish this was over." Taran's voice died away as her head went down on Thomas' shoulder and she slept.

"Did she really just do that?" Thomas looked up with a grin at Don.

"She did, Thomas. She didn't sleep at all last night. She was that worried about you." Don rose, leaving the couple on their own.

Thomas rose as well, gathering Taran close to his heart and finding an easy chair to sit in. He simply sat and held her as she slept before his head went down on her hair and he too slept. Rose and Rachel came looking for their children. Exchanging a glance, Rachel reached for a blanket and draped it over the two before they turned and walked away.

Don rose as well, heading for the rest of his team. They needed to meet for prayer. This was where it was becoming more dangerous for the couple.

Joshua turned from the window that he had been staring out of, a puzzled look on his face.

"Don? What's your take on this?"

"On this? You mean, Thomas disappearing and then reappearing?" Don thought that was what it was but he had to be sure.

"That. It doesn't make a whole lot of sense." Caleb spoke up from where he was working away, papers spread around him.

"No, it doesn't. We don't have that one piece of information that we need to solve this." Mark turned around from where he was working on his laptop. "So, how do we do this?"

"We work with what we have. You know, there is something that I'm trying to remember about George." Paul walked into the room, speaking to the others as he did so. "I just can't remember it. I wish I could. It's something to do with his family."

Chapter 27

Leaving the team working, Taran walked away from Don's home. She just kept walking, heading for her own home, knowing that Thomas would come looking for her. She felt smothered, just for now. Taran heard a vehicle approaching and darted away from the street, standing behind a tree. She sighed. Titus had come looking for her. She turned and walked away from the tree, ducking down another street.

Arriving at her home, Taran sank down into an office chair, her head buried in her arms on her desk. She had not realized that it was such a long walk. Her phone had been vibrating as she walked and she had ignored it. Taran wept as she huddled at the desk. She felt abandoned and terrified. She wanted this over but there didn't seem to be any end in sight.

Tam searched for his daughter at Don's before he headed for his truck. Thomas had looked around and then was on his feet, walking to where Tam was standing by his truck.

"Tam? Where's Taran?" Thomas had not missed her until then. That disturbed him.

"I have no idea. She's not here. I wonder?" Tam pointed at Thomas. "In." Tam drove off rapidly, Thomas not even getting a chance to buckle his seatbelt before Tam sped away.

"Tam? Where are we heading?" Thomas reached for his phone. Titus had sent a message, simply stating that he was trying to find Taran.

"Tell him to head for Taran's. I think that she likely walked home." Tam was worried about his daughter, afraid that she would disappear and they would never find her.

"Walked? Do you know how far that is?" Thomas sent off a text to Titus, sending him towards Taran's home.

"Walked. She would do that. It's not the first time that she has. She wouldn't want to bother or disturb anyone when we were deep in concentration." Tam sighed. It was a fact that his daughter was independent. He was proud of her for that but also deeply worried about her. He simply prayed for her.

Thomas was out of the truck, running towards the house, Tam beside him. Tam fumbled with his keys, dropping them multiple times before he found the lock with them and unlocked the door. He was into the house almost before the door had opened enough to let him. Thomas went one way in the house and Tam the other.

Hearing soft sobs, Thomas' feet slowed as he neared the office. He hesitated for a moment, not wanting to intrude on Taran's privacy before he was across the room. On his knees, Thomas swept her into his arms. Taran jumped as she felt the arms and then leaned against Thomas, her sobs deepening.

Tam stood beside the desk, his eyes on his daughter. Sorrow wafted through him as he heard her sobs. This was breaking her. All he could do is pray for her, asking for strength, protection and someone to defend her. He knew that God was there and had always been there. He also knew that sometimes a person needed someone on earth to walk with them. And for Taran, that person seemed to be Thomas. He turned away, finding Titus standing in the hallway.

"Tam? How did she get here?" Titus was confused.

"She walked. It's not the first time that she has done this. She doesn't want to take someone away from what they are doing. We've had to be stern with her many times over these decisions of hers." Tam rubbed at his face.

"I can see that." Titus watched his brother as he still knelt beside Taran. "They need each other. They're two parts of a whole."

"They are. We need to let them understand that themselves. God is here, Titus. He's watching for them." Tam turned away from his daughter and walked to the kitchen. His phone out, he sent a message off to Rachel, just to let her know where they were. He reached for the coffee pot to make fresh coffee.

Taran looked up at last, finding Thomas with his eyes closed as he prayed for her. She reached to touch his face, bringing his gaze to her.

"Taran? You walked?" Thomas was still in awe that she had but also worried about her.

"I did. I just needed to leave and be by myself. How did you know?"

"Your father. He's here. And I think that Titus is too."

———

"I see. Where are they?" Taran looked around Thomas. "Thomas? Where is God in all of this?"

"He's here, my darlin'. He's right here with us. He loves you so much that He only wants the best for you. He is working through this. We may not understand the why's here on earth but one day we will. For now, I am right here with you. Our families are. My team is. Our friends are. God is using each one of us. He has you sheltered in the hollow of His hand. He does not allow any harm to come to you that is not in His will."

Taran watched him closely. She nodded at last, her arms coming out to encircle Thomas' neck. He made her feel so safe. Only she was sure that when this was all over, he would just walk away from her.

Thomas kept his eyes on her head, knowing that she was struggling. He was as well. He knew his lady was hurting and that despite his medical skills, he could not heal her. Only God could do that.

"Thomas? Can I ask you something?" Taran didn't look at him. Her voice was still muffled against him.

"Anything, my darlin'. Anything." Thomas prayed for her, for her healing but also that she would always be a part of his life. He loved her, that much he had to acknowledge to himself.

"Where do we go from here?" Taran held her breath, almost afraid to breathe.

"Where do we go? As a couple?" Thomas felt her nod. "I would like to explore our friendship. See where it goes. I do not want to lose you even as a friend."

Taran felt herself relax. He didn't want to run from her after all. That she had been afraid of.

"Thank you, Thomas. You don't know what that means to me." Taran felt Thomas' kiss on her head.

"It means the same to me, I think. Listen. Your dad seems to have made coffee. And I am sure that Titus has found something to make for us to eat. How be we find them?"

Taran was on her feet, Thomas' arms still around her. He didn't release her, instead praying for them once more.

Tam turned as he felt a hand on his arm and simply hugged his daughter. He knew that the worse was yet to come for the couple. And that made him afraid. Tam released his daughter, his hands on her upper arms, his eyes watching her closely.

"You had to do that, didn't you?" He grinned at her, seeing her nod. "It's okay, love. I thought that you would have come home. But you should have asked for a ride. Any one of us would have done that."

"I know, Dad. I needed time by myself. And this is how I chose to do it. Only, it didn't work out so well." Taran scowled at him as he began to laugh. "It's not funny, Dad."

Tam continued to laugh, seeing the grins on the brothers' faces.

"I know it's not but it's just so you. You do this all the time, Taran."

"I know. And it not likely was a good choice. I should have asked for a ride. I just didn't want to disturb anyone." Taran's eyes were on Thomas, seeing understanding in his eyes.

"We get that, love, but for now, promise us that you will ask for a ride if you need it. You could disappear on us and we would never find you."

Chapter 28

Late that night, Thomas wandered his yard, not ready to sleep even though he was exhausted. He felt that he had to watch out for his lady. And he had acknowledged once more to himself that he was in love with her. He prayed for her, seeking protection and defense for her.

Hearing a noise, Thomas' steps slowed. His eyes searched through the darkness even as he backed away to stand near a tree at the back of the yard. He watched as two men snuck carefully through the yard, heading for the house. Thomas sighed. There would be no getting back into the house at this point. He stepped back further, heading for the woods behind him. Once he felt safe, Thomas pulled out his phone and called for help.

Waiting for the authorities to appear, Thomas' eyes narrowed. There was something off about this. He just didn't know what.

Thomas watched as the men exited the house right into the arms of the officers. He didn't move, knowing that the officers would search his home. Aidan appeared at his side, having received a text from Thomas.

"Thomas? You were outside?" Aidan's voice was low.

"I was. I couldn't sleep and was walking the yard. I heard something and moved back. They went right into the house. They seemed to know that I was not there." Thomas searched the area, his eyes stopping on a tree. "There. There's something in there, Aidan." Thomas ran that way, tackling the man who dropped down from the tree.

The man fought Thomas, a lucky blow landing across Thomas' eyes. Thomas moved back, blinking rapidly with a hand on his face. The man was on his feet, a foot viciously kicking out at Thomas' head, knocking him back to the ground where he lay still. Spinning, the man stopped, his hands rising in the air. Aidan stood there, his weapon pointed at the man, other officers surrounding the trio.

Aidan shoved the man towards an officer. Handcuffed, the man was led away to join his cohorts in custody. He then turned to the officer attending to Thomas. He sighed. This was not how it was to be. Aidan turned away, walking towards Thomas' house. He knew that he had to call Taran. Instead of calling her, he headed for his car.

Taran rose from where she had been curled up on the couch. She squinted at the clock in the low light that she had on. Just after midnight, she thought. Who would be here at this time of night?

Aidan pulled Taran with him, stuffing her into his car. He knew that someone would have reached out to Thomas' family. This was not what they needed.

"Aidan? What happened? It is Thomas or my parents?" Taran was scared, almost terrified.

"It's Thomas. Someone tried to abduct him tonight. I won't go into all the details but he was hurt. I'll get you to him." Aidan watched the traffic around him closely, knowing that he was being followed. "Hang tight, Taran. We have a tail and I need to lose it."

Aidan spun his wheel and stepped on the accelerator. He sped away, turning onto streets that he knew would lead him towards the hospital. He just could not shake his tail. Calling for help, Aidan hit the sirens and lights and sped through the darkened streets away from the hospital and towards the police department. He prayed that they would make it in time but there were no guarantees that would happen.

Taran grew more afraid as moments passed. She didn't dare ask Aidan any questions. She didn't want to distract him. All Taran would do was beg God to keep them safe. She didn't know if they would make it to wherever it was that Aidan was heading.

Slowing to make his turn into the parking lot, Aidan was grateful as the gates slid open and then closed behind him. Out of his vehicle, his hand reached for Taran's, pulling her towards the back of the building. The door opened and Aidan dove through, shoving Taran ahead of him.

Stumbling as she tried to catch her balance, Taran spun to stare at Aidan, not quite sure what was happening.

Not speaking, Aidan directed Taran to his office and then shoved her into a chair. He was away and back with bottles of water. Taran took the one handed to her and sipped from it. She was more shaken than she wanted to admit.

<hr>

Aidan was out of his office again, searching for an officer who he could send to be with Thomas. He was afraid that someone would make another attempt on him in the hospital.

Thaddeus and Rose stood near Thomas' stretcher, their eyes on their son. He had not roused as yet. The physician was not worried, they knew, feeling that he would soon rouse.

"He'll have bruising on his face, Thaddeus. He took quite a blow. I'll be around if you have any questions." The physician walked away, not sure what to say. He paused and turned once more, hearing other footsteps.

Don stood nearby, his gaze shifting from the physician to Thomas' room. The physician simply shook his head and walked away. Don stared at him, knowing that something was off about him. He sent a text to Emma, asking her to investigate that physician. He may or may not be involved in what was happening but his reaction just now was not expected.

Rose looked around as Don approached.

"Don? Who called you?"

"One of the officers did. I need to be here for all of you. How is he?" Don winced as he saw the bruise on Thomas' face.

"He's not waking yet, Don. And I think that he should." Rose controlled her emotions with difficulty, Thaddeus' arm around her. "Who did this?"

"I'm not sure. I don't have a lot of information yet. Aidan said they were still working the scene but that they had his assailant in custody. Apparently, there was an abduction attempt tonight." Don watched with compassion as Rose's fears for her son surfaced before she could control them.

"Taran? Where is she?" Thaddeus had expected her to appear by now.

"She's with Aidan. He was headed here but instead took her to the department." Don had been dismayed at what Aidan had told him.

"She's safe. That's the main thing. This is just going to get worse, isn't it?" Thaddeus didn't expect a response. There was none needed. They all knew that it would indeed get much worse. They just prayed that the couple would survive without harm or injury.

Chapter 29

Taran rose at last, pacing Aidan's office. She was puzzled at what had happened to them. To think that whoever it was had dared to try and take an officer captive? Taran didn't understand that. It just didn't seem to fit with what they had gone through.

"Aidan? This doesn't make sense. Who was chasing us tonight?" Taran turned to face him, her hands resting on the back of the chair that she had just been sitting in.

"I don't know, Taran. I couldn't get much of a description. They stayed back just far enough so that I couldn't in the dark. And if we don't have that, then we don't know who to watch out for."

"I get that, Aidan." Taran's voice stopped. "Have you heard any word on Thomas?"

"He's still out of it, Taran. Other than a bruise, Thaddeus said there was no other injury that they could see. His jaw is bruised but not broken." Aidan watched with compassion as her face crumpled for a moment.

"That's good. I need to see him, Aidan. Can we go there?" Taran turned and paced once more, unable to sit still.

"We'll get you there, Taran." Aidan bit at his lip. He needed to ask Taran something but he didn't know quite how to do that. "Taran? I need to ask you something. And if you don't want to answer, that's okay. Just how close are you two?"

___

Taran had turned as he spoke. She nodded. He would need to know that. It would help keep them safe.

"I'm not sure what you're asking but we are talking, Aidan. This, whatever you want to call it, is getting in the way. We are planning on dating." Taran sat back down, her eyes closing against her emotions.

"And we'll get you there. If he's released before I can leave here, then we'll take you to wherever he is." Aidan was on his feet as he saw an officer beckoning to him. "George?"

"Thomas' attacker is talking. He doesn't know a lot. He was just hired to watch from the tree as the other two went in. One of them hired him." George was frustrated.

"I see. Get what information you can from him and then send him back to a cell. We'll take it to the crown attorney and see what they want to do. In the meantime, I need to get Taran to Thomas."

"How is Thomas? He took quite a blow from what I heard." George moved to where he could watch Taran.

"He did. But he was moving backward to some extent when the foot connected with his jaw. That saved him from a fractured jaw." Aidan watched Taran as well. "I need to get her to him."

"There are officers waiting to do that, Aidan. If you can leave in about fifteen minutes, they'll be all set." George walked away, leaving Aidan staring at the floor, a thoughtful look on his face.

There has to be something that we're missing, he decided. *I just don't know what it is. Lord, this would be a good time for You to give me a hint. I need that. We have no information that is new that will help. Even what is being sent to us isn't solving this. Please, Lord? Just a touch of Your hand on this to solve this.*

Walking into the hospital, Aidan kept a hand on Taran's upper arm. He didn't want her to get too far from him and he was afraid that was what she would do in her haste to get to Thomas. Showing his identification, Aidan walked into the Emergency Department, Taran tight to his side. He paused at the doorway to Thomas' room, seeing Thomas sitting upright on the stretcher.

Taran gave a soft sound that was just loud enough for Thomas to hear her. His arm came out as she ran towards him, sweeping her close to him. His parents had left, knowing that he wanted that. He would be released in a few hours and would head their way at that point. He knew that Don was around as was Mark.

Aidan approached, his footsteps slow and cautious. He studied Thomas and then Taran before he nodded. They're a couple, he thought.

"Aidan? What can you tell me? I don't remember much." Thomas winced at the pain from speaking.

"Not a lot. The man who attacked you had been hired just to climb that tree and watch for you."

"That's strange. Tell me that he gave a name." Thomas didn't expect Aidan to be able to give a name but he could still hope. He wanted this over. He could feel the fear shaking his lady as he hugged her to him.

"He didn't. He's not saying much other than that. We're working on it, Thomas. We just don't know when this will end. And when I was bringing Taran here, we were followed." Aidan's face was stern.

Thomas stared at him and then down at his lady. This is not what he wanted to hear, not at all. God had protected her, he knew. His team, he also knew, had gathered outside in the waiting room, ready to protect and defend him and Taran. It had come to that time, he decided.

Don walked into the room at that point, hesitating for a moment. He locked his gaze with Thomas and then nodded. It had come to that, he knew. Emma and Abe were on their way from Riverville. They just had to decide where to put Thomas and Taran.

Taran turned as she heard Don's footsteps. She knew that it had come to crunch time as was said. She was not prepared to go into hiding. She couldn't. Her staff and customers were relying on her and she would not disappoint them.

"I'm not going into hiding." Taran didn't surprise the three men. They had expected that from her. "So, how do we do this?"

"We work with you, Taran. I find someone to be with you at the store. Richard and his team will help as will Abe and his team. Our team is there for you. You will be escorted back and forth to work. I'm sorry

that you'll lose your freedom for now. It's either that
or lose your life." Don knew Taran well enough that
he had to be honest with her. She would take nothing
less than that.

Taran nodded. She had come to that conclusion.
She just prayed that this would be over soon. It was
getting to be too close to home as her mother would
have said. She wanted to get on with her life and
couldn't.

Chapter 30

Moving through her store the next morning, Taran was not at peace. She had spent a long time the night before in prayer, begging God to end this. It just didn't seem that it would end very soon. That disappointed her but also scared her. Taran knew that this was where it got dangerous. No one had to tell her that. Thomas had been reluctant to leave her that morning. Mark and Thomas had escorted her to work, Mark staying with her.

Mark watched the customers and staff moving through the store over the day. He appreciated the fact of how fair and kind that Taran was to her staff. They worked together as a team, which is what he had come to expect from her.

Taran sighed as the day ended. She finished off her end-of-day procedures and then locked away what needed to be. Walking towards Mark, her feet seemed reluctant to move. Someone was outside, she felt, and meant them harm. She came to a stop in the middle of the store.

Turning from where he had been waiting, Mark studied her and then moved to study the outside. The doors were locked and he had no intention of unlocking them. He too could feel something off and that meant that someone was outside. He had learned to trust his instincts and his feelings.

"Mark? Someone is out there. I can't go out either door." Taran spun in a circle, not sure where to go. "What do we do?"

"We call for help." Mark's phone was out as he called Don, simply asking for the team to come. There seemed to be danger outside and he was not prepared to take Taran out of the door on his own. Pocketing his phone, he moved through the store before he was back beside Taran. "Don and the rest will come. For now, where can we go?"

Taran shrugged. She had no idea where they could go or where they would be safe.

"I don't know, Mark."

Banging at the back door had Taran uttering a small scream and jumping. Mark's hand was on her arm, heading for the office. He shoved her inside and then shut and locked the door. His hand was on his weapon. Someone was trying to break in and he didn't think that his team would be there in time. Mark knew that he would do his best to protect Taran. He just didn't know if it would be enough.

Thomas stared at the broken-in back door before he moved forward. Joshua and Caleb's hands on his arms stopped in. He nodded, knowing that the police had to move in first.

Aidan approached the building, knowing that Taran was not inside. Mark was down and injured. The paramedics were waiting to move in to tend to him. They just had to wait until the building was cleared.

Joe approached Don, beckoning him to one side.

"Don? I received word of a break-in. I tried to get here as soon as I could. Taran?" Joe kept his eyes on the building.

"I don't know, Joe. Mark called us to come and escort her home. By the time that we arrived, the door was broken in." Don kept watching Thomas, knowing that Thomas would be in the building and searching for his lady as soon as he could.

Aidan walked towards Thomas who kept his eyes on him, hope still on his face. His face dropped as did his head. Aidan's smile was sad. Taran was not there. Mark was down and injured. They would be moving him off shortly for care.

"Thomas? Taran's not there. Mark is hurt. What happened?"

"I don't know. I had a text from her about two hours ago, just responding to one of mine. We planned on going out for a meal at Ben's. Then, Mark called Don, asking for us to appear. We did. She's not there?" Thomas was praying that he had heard Aidan wrong.

"No, I'm sorry, Thomas. She's not. I can't let you inside. You know that." Aidan looked around. "Joe? I'll walk you through once the team is done. You can tell me if anything is missing."

Aidan walked away, finding Toryn standing nearby.

"How bad, Aidan?" Toryn knew that it was. He could tell by the way Aidan was moving.

"Bad enough, Toryn. Mark? He took a bullet to his abdomen. They'll take him in shortly. Taran seems to have put up a fight. The office is a mess." Aidan sighed. This was not how this was to be going. "Where is God, Toryn?"

"God is here, Aidan. It's hard to trust at times, I know. I've been where you are right now many times. He's here in our midst. He's with Mark, waiting to heal him. He's with Thomas and their families as they will need to wait for word. He's with Taran wherever it is that she is. We'll find her."

"I know that we'll find her. I just don't know if she'll still be alive or not." Aidan drew in a deep breath. "There was a letter left, Toryn, addressed to you. I had the team bag it for now. We'll look at it when we get back to the department."

Toryn looked surprised for a moment before he nodded. Aidan had made the right decision.

"That's fair. I'm heading back that way. Find me when you return." Toryn walked away, a slight slump to his shoulders. This was not what he wanted to hear. He prayed for the couple, knowing that Thomas would be out there, hunting for Taran, and putting himself at risk.

Tam and Rachel were shocked when Aidan appeared. They had spoken with Taran over the lunch hour. To hear that she was missing was not what they had expected.

"She's missing? How?" Tam wanted details, knowing that he not likely would get all of them that he wanted.

"We don't know for sure. She disappeared from her store. We're working out from it, as well always do. Did she say anything at all?" Aidan was praying that she had and he could go and find her.

"Not a word. We talked about what we wanted to do on Sunday as a family. Other than that it was just everyday stuff." Rachel leaned against Tam, her heart breaking for her daughter. "Thomas? How is he?"

"He's hurting, Rachel. Mark was with Taran today. He's been injured and is receiving treatment." Aidan stayed for a while longer before he left. He stood beside his car, his eyes raising to the night sky. The stars and moon seemed extra bright and large that night. A promise from God, he decided, that God was there, a light in their darkness. He smiled before he was driving away, heading for the department and Toryn.

———

Chapter 31

A week had passed. Mark was home once more, healing. He was devastated that he had been unable to protect Taran. The men had been on them before he could react. The bullet had found him too quickly for him to pull his own weapon. To hear that Taran was still missing was not what Mark needed to hear.

Thomas paced the office during the day, doing what he needed to. He was losing weight, his tan fading. Dark circles under his eyes were showing darker each day. He spent time with his family and with Taran's. They were all trying to make sense of what had happened and why. Titus and Thomas had taken to driving around town during the evening, knowing that his team was doing the same. One of his team members was usually with him.

Payten had taken over making meals for the team as they struggled to work and then investigate. Richard and his team had taken to showing up when they could to help search. Don knew that they were investigating as well. Abe and Emma had been around. Thomas knew that Abe's team and his friends were in town at odd hours, all searching for his lady.

Paul and Thomas made their way on that following Saturday towards Ben's. Neither man was really interested in a meal. They were just hoping that Ben had word.

Ben watched Thomas closely before he pointed towards his office. Paul nodded, a hand on Thomas' shoulder sending him that way. He waited for Ben to speak.

"Paul? Any word?" Ben stopped in the hallway, away from the bustle and noise of the kitchen.

"Not a word. We're looking everywhere that we can. Our friends are looking, even coming in from out of town to do so." Paul sighed. "We don't know where she is. We're trusting God in this but it is hard. I remember what it felt like."

Ben nodded. He had spoken with both Toryn and Aidan, asking what he could do to help. Word was out on the street that Thomas' Taran was missing. Ben had spoken with various leaders of the groups there. No one had any word. That was puzzling to them all.

Thomas approached them, his phone in his hand. He was puzzled by the text messages that he had just been receiving. Abe's business partner, Murphy, had been in touch, asking questions that he was unable to answer.

"Paul? Is there an abandoned house near the lake that isn't in too bad of shape?" Thomas knew of a few that might fit that description.

"There are a few. Why?" He told Thomas' phone and read the messages. "Where does he get this?"

"Emma. She finds these places, you know. I wonder if Taran is in one of them." Thomas stood, not sure what to do or where to go.

———

Ben's hand shoved him back towards the office before he reached for the tray being handed to him. He followed the two younger men, setting the tray down.

"Eat, Thomas. Paul. Eat and then we pray. Let me know the address that Murphy is asking about." Ben took the slip of paper and walked away, standing in the hallway to watch the two. He glanced down at the address and froze. He knew the house and he knew who owned it. If Taran was in that man's hands, he feared for her life. Ben had heard the rumours over the years of the evilness of the man and of the people who had been in his orbit and simply vanished.

Aidan walked in at that point, finding Ben still staring at the paper. He frowned before he reached for it, taking it from Ben's fingers. He studied the address.

"Ben? What is this?" Aidan's voice was kept low, not disturbing the men in the office.

"Murphy sent this address to Thomas. Emma found this address and sent it on." Ben nodded towards the men. "They'll want to go out there."

"And they can't. They need to leave that to us." Aidan walked away, the slip of paper tucked into his shirt pocket. He needed to be downtown for now, an investigation that was demanding his attention.

Ben watched Aidan leave before he turned back to the office, sitting at his desk. He watched Thomas closely before he nodded. Thomas will go out there whether he should or not.

"Don't do it, Thomas. Don't go out there." Ben's voice was quiet and calm. "Aidan was just here

———

and has the address. He'll investigate it. We can't do anything that would compromise his investigation."

Thomas nodded, knowing that Ben was correct. That was exactly what he wanted to do and couldn't.

"What do we do then, Ben? How do we investigate that place?" Paul spoke up, knowing from experience that Ben would have an idea of how to do that.

"We'll investigate it, Paul. How be I head for your place late this afternoon? We'll meet there. No one would think anything of me doing that, not given our relationship." Ben and his wife had taken Paul into their homes after he had been injured on the streets.

"We can do that. Payten will welcome your help with a meal." Paul grinned at Ben who simply grinned back and shook his head. "Come on, Thomas. Let's find the families and our team and make some plans. I know that some of Richard's team was heading this way today. We'll meet at my place this afternoon. In the meantime, we can do some research on our own."

Thomas nodded, his eyes dropping to the mug that he held. He was hurting for himself but hurting more for his lady. He couldn't walk in and save her. He just didn't know for sure where she was. That was something that everyone was working on. Only no one seemed sure about where Taran was being held.

Late that night, Thomas turned from locking the door behind his friends. Titus was still there, insisting that he needed to stay. Thomas had merely nodded, knowing that his brother would stay whether he said he could or not.

Aidan had left earlier than the others, seeking out Toryn. They were both puzzled about the letter that had been left in the pharmacy. It didn't make a lot of sense, they had decided. There were no demands, no comment as to why Taran was taken. It was simply a note that said whoever had her would be in touch. And the investigation needed to stop.

Dropping his keys on his home office desk, Aidan yawned and then stretched. He was exhausted, he decided, and then headed for his bed. His prayers were for those who were his friends and also for the cases that he was working on. There were many at the time. The detectives all felt overworked and at a loss with some of those very cases.

God, please bring Taran home and safe and well. Thomas needs her. He's hurting in so many ways, dear Lord. We know the words and the promises. It's just hard when it's a friend going through this. It hurt with Paul and now with Thomas. And somehow, I think that it will go through all of our friends on that team. I just pray for Your protection on them and Your defense of them.

Chapter 32

Taran paced the house that she was locked into. It was not a well-cared for house, that much she knew. The walls needed to be repainted. The floors were rough, although clean. She had enough blankets to keep her warm. Taran just wanted to leave and couldn't. There were two of her abductors with her at all times, one in the house and one outside. At night, the bedroom door was locked.

She sighed to herself. A week had gone by, a long, lonely week. She prayed for Thomas and hoped that he was well. She feared for Mark, seeing in her mind the blood on his body as he fell under the onslaught of the men. She had fought them, trying desperately to escape and unable to free her wrist from the iron grasp of the man who dragged her from the building. Sobs had risen inside her and she had fought to keep them down.

Standing in the kitchen, Taran studied the room. It was not a kitchen that she would work in much, she knew. The flooring and countertops were worn and broken in pieces. She was forced to prepare meals for them all, one of the men standing in the kitchen watching carefully. She was only allowed sharp knives when meals were under preparation and then they were removed.

That night, Taran threw herself on the bed, her eyes staring at the curtainless window. She knew in her heart that her time in that house was near an end. She just didn't know if she would survive or not and whether she would walk towards her family and Thomas or if they would find her in a funeral home somewhere.

Her eyes closed as tears trickled down her face. She had given into her despair and the tears were flowing from her heart. She knew that God was there. She had felt His hand on her during the week. Her thoughts had turned to the verses that she had memorized and seemed to forget until then. God was refreshing her memory with them. Taran clung to the promise that God would never leave her and that He loved her. She slept at last, feeling peace coming from God filling her heart. She didn't hear the calls of the men who were on guard or the footsteps that approached the bedroom.

The lock was opened and a man appeared in the room, his shadow showing black on the wall across from the bed. He moved quietly towards Taran, finding her asleep. He simply lifted her into his arms, her arm coming around his neck, and turned, heading for the outdoors and the vehicles that awaited them. They were inside and leaving, four men with Taran and the other four staying with their prisoners.

Aidan roused as he heard his phone, sighing. He was not on call so he had no idea who would be calling him. Blinking, he stared at the text message before the blankets were thrown back and then he dressed rapidly. He ran for his vehicle, heading for the lake and the men waiting for him.

Abe Finlay turned as he heard a vehicle, walking towards Aidan. They shook hands before Abe pointed behind him.

———

"We talked with Toryn and a judge. They had a search warrant in play for us. We have Taran, Aidan." Age watched as Aidan's eyes slid closed before they popped open again.

"She's okay?" Aidan was worried about her.

"She was sleeping, Matt said, and didn't rouse when he picked her up to carry her out. They'll take her to Thomas." Abe pointed towards the men in handcuffs. "We have these two for you. I called for a patrol officer. Toryn has been in touch. He's sending a crime scene team as well, he said."

"He is? Good. Now, talk to me, Abe. How did you know?"

Abe shrugged. Emma had found the information and she couldn't explain how.

"Emma. She found this place and asked us to go in. It was confirmed that she was here. She can't give that information as to how she found it."

"We know that, Abe. We're just grateful that Taran is home." Aidan walked towards the house, stopping by the patrol officer who had responded. "Trevor? We have help on the way. Abe's team will wait with us until our teams are on site."

Abe walked away at last, heading for the SUV that was waiting for him. Joseph nodded towards the building, a question on his face, as Abe sat in the front passenger's seat and fastened his seatbelt.

"We're set to go?"

"We are. Thanks, guys. Another lady at home with her family. We know what it's like." Abe drew

———

in a deep breath. His team had been through difficulties and dangers with their ladies as had a number of their friends.

"Have you heard from Matt?" Nathaniel spoke up from the back seat.

"No, I haven't. We're heading that way so hopefully we'll find out how she is." Abe was tired. There had been too many friends who had been through this. He wondered when it would end.

Thomas turned as he heard a tapping at the door. He shared a look with Titus before he headed to open it, surprised to see four of Abe's men standing there. His eyes dropped as Matt moved forward. His hand on Matt's arm stopped his forward motion.

"Taran? She's here?" Thomas was shocked to say the least.

"She's here, Thomas. We found her. Now, where can I place her? We need to have a physician come in and assess her." Matt followed Thomas as he headed for the spare room to throw back the blankets on the bed.

Matt gently placed Taran on the bed before he pulled the covers over her and stepped back out of the room. His compassionate gaze was on Thomas who had dropped to his knees beside the bed, an arm around his lady and his head buried against her. It would take time, Matt knew, for them to feel safe and secure again. And Abe's team would provide the support that was needed.

———

Titus had watched closely as Taran had been carried into the house before he turned to the other three. His mouth opened and then snapped closed. He would not ask the questions that hovered on the tip of his tongue. Those answers had to come from Aidan. He simply pointed to the kitchen.

"She's okay?" Titus just had to ask.

"She is. She's sleeping, Titus. We'll have a physician come in and assess her." Luke reached for the coffee pot, comfortable enough to do that.

"I know that you will. What can I do to help?" Titus reached for bread and sandwich material, squinting at the clock. "We'll need to call her family and our family as well as Don and the team."

"We've done that, Titus. They're waiting for morning to come. Her parents are waiting for an officer to bring them. Aidan arranged for that." Micah reached to help with the sandwiches.

Chapter 33

Rousing hours later, Taran didn't dare open her eyes. She sensed that she was somewhere else and that terrified her. She had not felt herself being moved. Her eyes finally opened a little bit and she stared around. A breath of relief came from her. She was at Thomas' place. Just how she had arrived there, she was not sure.

On her feet, Taran found clean clothes waiting for her. They were her own clothes. That puzzled her for a moment before she shrugged. She showered and dressed in clean clothes for the first time in a week. Hesitating, Taran's head was bowed and she thanked God for His defense of her and her release from captivity. She could feel the freedom that God wanted for her once more. She knew that there was still danger but Taran also knew that God was in control. She could feel His presence once more.

Thomas looked up from where he was leaning against a wall in the hallway. His arms simply opened up as Taran spotted him and then launched herself towards him. He tightened his grip on her, feeling the shudders of her emotions shaking her body. He could relate to that. His emotions were raw as well.

Titus stood in the kitchen doorway, his eyes on his brother. Rachel stood beside him, an arm around the young man. Taran was back with Thomas, who loved her deeply he had finally admitted to them the night before. They just had to find out who was responsible and bring them to justice.

Taran looked around, seeing her mother waiting for her. She almost rand to be gathered into her mother's arms, sobs shaking her body. She had been told that she would never see her family again and that had almost destroyed her.

Tam looked up from the table, on his feet to wrap his ladies in his arms. Titus walked away towards his brother.

"Thomas? What now?" Titus finally asked the question that was needing to be asked.

"We solve this. We find the men responsible and bring them to justice. That's what we work on. We're getting closer. There is one piece of information that we need that is missing. What is it?"

"That house where she was? Do we know who owns it?" Titus was thinking through what they knew.

"Not that I am aware of." Thomas reached for his phone, sending out a text message to a friend. "Samuel will research it for us. Knowing him, he will make it a priority." Samuel was a title searcher in Elmton and was a friend of theirs. His wife, Aideen, had been a close friend of Paul's when they were teenagers.

"That he will. Now, let's eat. Tam wants to spend time in prayer. And I know that Mom and Dad and your team will be here within the hour."

"That they will be. Don was sorting through the information that we have already found and will bring it with him. We don't have any teams in for training next week. Instead, we'll work this." Thomas stared towards his office. "We need to put paper up on the walls, Titus." He turned to head that way, a hand on his arm stopping him.

"Wait, Thomas. We eat first and then we pray. We need to bathe you and Taran in prayer. With her getting away as she did last night? They'll come after you even harder." Titus watched his brother closely.

Thomas paused before he nodded. He was exhausted, fatigue weighing down his body and his thoughts. He knew that it was only the strength that came from God that was getting him through this. He walked towards Taran, an arm around her as he headed them for the kitchen.

Two hours later, the office buzzed with conversation and some laughter. Both families and the team were at work. Titus and Caleb had worked on putting blank newsprint paper on the wall while Joshua and Mark worked at jotting down what they had found. Taran watched them, amazed at how much information they had already discovered.

Aidan had been around, taking her statement. He had simply shaken his head at her at the question in her eyes. She had nodded herself, knowing that he could not or would not tell her what was happening. He couldn't as it was an active investigation. Aidan had walked away, heading for the department to see what he could discover. There was just that one piece of information missing that they could not determine. Toryn was waiting for him, pointing to his own office. He closed the door, intending on spending time in prayer with his detective and friend.

———

Thaddeus had read all that was on the papers taped to the walls and then walked outside. He needed solitude to think it over. There was something all too familiar about what he was reading. Thaddeus had an idea who it was and that troubled him more than anything had ever troubled him. If it was the man who he suspected, Thaddeus knew him to be a friend or acquaintance. He had not suspected him at all. Tam approached him, giving a name. Thaddeus looked at him in surprise and then nodded. Both fathers knew who was behind it now. They just had to find the information that was needed. They just didn't know how to do that.

Don had followed, just standing to watch Thaddeus. He approached him at last, a question asked. Thaddeus had stared at him and then nodded. Don sighed. Thaddeus had just comforted his suspicions. It would take work to prove that it was this man and more than likely his family. How they did that was a question neither of the men had answers for.

Walking back to the house, Don had found his team. He spoke quietly to them and sent them out to search the downtown area and the area around his business. Titus had volunteered to go with the five, knowing that they would work better in pairs. Don had been grateful for his assistance.

Taran had watched the men walk away, a question on her lips that died as she watched Thomas watching her. He had approached her, a kiss dropped on her forehead, before he prayed for her and then walked away. Fear rose inside her as she saw that action. She was afraid for him and the team with him.

———

179

Daci simply stood beside her friend, an arm wrapped around her. Titus stood on her other side, tall and strong, determined to protect his brother's lady. Only none of them know just how to do that.

Rachel and Rose had approached Taran, drawing her away from the office and into the kitchen. They would need to cook and bake, they informed her, and they needed her help. Their quiet conversation and joking around had helped to ease her worry. She still looked frequently at the door, willing Thomas and the other five men to return.

Chapter 34

Thomas stood in the conference room, not sure where he was to be. His heart was in his home with Taran but his mind was here in the office. He looked around as Paul spoke.

"Thomas? What are your thoughts? Both of us are from this town. Who would you suspect?" Paul set his phone down on the table, knowing that Thomas had been thinking about who.

"Who? Who would we least expect?" Thomas turned to sit on the edge of the table, one foot swinging freely as he did so. His arms crossed across his chest. His eyes didn't leave his friend's face.

"That's what we always think, isn't it? We've listed a number of names. I don't think that's who it is. Who's the most obvious?" Paul headed for the whiteboard on the wall and reached for a black marker. He turned as the others entered. "Don? Who would you most suspect?"

Don stopped by the chair that he usually chose. His eyes narrowed as he thought through what Paul was asking. He nodded at that, watching Mark, Joshua, and Caleb. These three men were raised in the neighbouring small towns or villages.

"I see what you mean, Paul. We usually list who is the least suspected." Don thought through the town. "There are always rumours about certain men. Paul, Ben has sent a text." He reached for his phone to retrieve the message. He read it out, giving the name that Ben had suggested.

Paul and Thomas shared a look before they both nodded. That would likely be who it was.

"That's him, Don." Thomas sighed, knowing that it affected not only himself and his family but the team as well.

"That's who I was thinking of as well, Don." Paul wrote the man's name on the whiteboard and then began listing the family who they knew.

Mark's phone was out as he sent off a text message to Emma. She responded immediately, simply stating that he could expect information emailed to him shortly. Mark headed for a computer and pulled up his email program. The email from Emma was there. He printed off the information that she had sent and handed it around.

Joshua and Caleb read through it before they raised their heads. They knew of this man but not his name. He had been seen in their home area and when he did, crime happened. Don was standing nearby them by that time and reached for the material that Mark was handing out. He frowned for a moment before he nodded. This was the man.

"Okay, people. We know who it is. Let's see what we can do to prove it. I am sure that Emma has sent this on to Aidan." Don looked around as Mark made a sound.

Mark was shaking his head, causing Don to frown at him once more.

"She hasn't yet. She wants to prove a little bit more information and then she will. She sent it to us so that we can be prepared and watch for him. She has given a number of associates and employees." Mark flipped to the third page. "Here's the list. And we know most of them."

Paul paled as he read the list, knowing most of them.

"We know them, guys. Some of them have been through here in training in the last couple of weeks. What did we do?"

Don paled as well. He read through the list. Paul was right. At least six had been through there in the last few weeks. How had their investigation of them failed?

"How did we not see this? We did our investigation of them." Don turned to Mark. "I know that you did as thorough an investigation into them as we could."

"I did, Don. Let me go through this with Emma. For now, I'm sending her the names of everyone we have coming through. We can't take a chance. If these men got through, then who knows who else will." Mark walked away, heading for his office, intent on speaking with Emma. It dismayed and frustrated him that the men had gotten through the barriers that they had set up.

Thomas had been listening to the conversation even as he stared down at the paperwork. He drew in a deep breath. This involved more than just Taran and himself. It also involved their fathers, his at least. He knew that Thaddeus had had issues with the man named.

"Don? I don't think that it's Taran and me that they're after. I think it's our fathers. Dad has had run-ins with this man, most recently about six months ago. He tried to take over Dad's business and Dad had to get a restraining order against him. Dad's business is landscaping as you know. We couldn't figure out why they wanted his business." Thomas looked up as Joshua stopped beside him.

"And Taran's father? He's an optometrist. How would that work into crime?" Joshua was puzzled. He walked away, his phone out to call Tam.

"This is bizarre, you know." Caleb paced, a hand rubbing at his cheek. He didn't see the table and comfortable chairs that sat around it nor did he take in the framed photographs and prints that lined the cream walls. He was lost in thought, trying to make sense of it all. Only he couldn't.

Mark returned, a stern look on his face. He handed a sheet of paper to Don who took in his look. Don's heart sank. Something more had happened. He read Mark's notes before he drew in a deep breath.

"Guys? Emma has found the link between the fathers. It is this man but it goes deeper. It goes back to their fathers and his father. How do we do this now? We need to think this through." Don was in his chair, pulling a pad of paper and pen towards him. He heard the chairs moving back as all but Joshua sat.

Joshua was back, a tray of mugs and the coffee pot on it. He set it down, handing around the filled mugs and then the plates of sandwiches. Rose had dropped over with food for them, knowing that they would be deep into their investigations.

Don bowed his head, the men following suit, as they prayed for their friends, the families, and then Aidan and his team as they investigated this. They were well aware that only God would and could solve this in a reasonable amount of time. They petitioned for protection for Thomas and Taran and that God would defend them against their enemies.

Chapter 35

Thomas rose from his chair, walking towards the white board. Consulting the papers that he held, he updated his work. Standing back, he read through it all and then nodded. It was starting to come together. They would continue to work it as they were able. For now, they needed to take a break. Don stood beside him, nodding as well.

"We've done good work today, Thomas. It's coming together. Emma is working through this as well. Go on. Find your lady. She's liking looking for you." Don gave a smile as Thomas nodded and then walked away, the papers that he had been working on dropped on the desk in his office.

Heading for his truck, Thomas waited for a moment before he put the truck into gear and drove off. He didn't see the patrol car following him. Aidan had arranged for that.

The team members walked away, heading off to their own activities. They were concerned for Thomas and Taran. Don watched as the team left before he turned back into the office and to the boardroom. His phone was out as he took photos of the white boards. He needed to speak with Aidan but he knew that Aidan was away until Monday. He would need to wait to do that. For the next week, Don had to decide what his team did. He sat at his desk, pulling his work schedule towards him. He worked away for a while before he was on his feet and heading for his own home. He had a meeting to get to but just wasn't in the mood for it.

———

Taran turned as she heard Thomas' voice, knowing that he had returned to his home, safe and sound. She waited for him to approach her. Thomas wrapped her into his arms, a kiss delivered to her forehead.

"Okay, my darlin'?" Thomas simply held her, feeling her relaxing against him.

"I am. And you?" Taran waited for him to speak, knowing that he would when he was ready.

"I am. We've managed to determine who it is. We just don't know why." Thomas knew that both sets of parents were still there. He could heard his father's footsteps stopping nearby. "Dad, we know who it is." Thomas gave the name, hearing the sharp intake of his father's breath.

"Him? Tam? Have you had problems with him?" Thaddeus turned to Tam, seeing his nod.

"I have. Are we the cause of the trouble that these two have been going through?" Tam was devastated at the thought.

"It might be. We think that it goes back to his father and Grandpa, Dad, and to your father, Tam." Thomas turned to face them, keeping an arm around his lady.

"It does. He was very clear about that, son." Thaddeus thought through the issues and words that the man had had with him. "It goes back to Dad. You know that I took over Dad's business. His father didn't like that. He wanted Dad's business. We could never figure out why." He looked up at his son, standing tall and strong in front of him. He wondered where the years had gone, thinking back to the toddler, then child, and then teen who had worked with him in his business.

"Emma's looking into that. She had an idea that she was running with. She said she'd get back to us as soon as she could. Now, we have to figure out how to draw him out and have Aidan arrest him." Thomas thought through what they could do but had no firm idea.

"Dad? Why would he want your business? You're an optometrist. What crime could be involved in that?" Taran watched her father, seeing as he had a thought.

"Smuggling, love. We receive supplies from all over. If he put someone into the office or took over the whole practice, he could bring in objects that would never be discovered. There were always rumours about his father being involved in crime but we could never prove it." Tam shared a look with Thomas. "It looks as if you two are the ones who will do that." He walked away, his shoulders slumping. He didn't like that his daughter had to face this monster as he called him.

That evening, Ben watched as Thomas led Taran into the diner and to a booth near the kitchen. He also watched as two men followed them in, choosing a table near the front of the diner where they could watch the couple. They were not just here for a meal, he decided, before he walked over to Thomas.

"Thomas. Taran. You're here for a meal?" He grinned at them before he sobered. "Thomas, the two men seated at the front of the diner? They followed you two in. What I am about to suggest is that you two come with me. I'll set you up in a room that I use for special parties." He waited for the couple to rise and then led them from the diner to a room near his office.

Taran was surprised at that, not knowing that this was Ben. Thomas simply thanked Ben and seated Taran at a table. He looked around, knowing that Ben had likely read the situation correctly. He decided that he would speak with Ben about the man who they suspected but that would not happen that night. Tonight was about being out with his lady.

Walking out through the kitchen, Thomas kept Taran's hand tight in his. Ben was watching the men, ready to call for help if he needed to. He nodded at Thomas' thanks, knowing that he would have done a lot more for the man. Don's team were good friends, part because of Paul and part because of who they were. He prayed for them daily, knowing that they had dangerous work.

Taran sighed as she walked back through her home that night. She felt that she was doing that a lot lately. Her heart was constantly begging God to end this and let her live her life as He had planned. She had no doubt that Thomas would be a part of it. She was just afraid that something would happen to him and she would lose him. Taran knew that Thomas had that concern for her.

Hearing her phone chiming, Taran reached for it. It was Titus, just saying good night to his future sister-in-law. A smiling face emoji accompanied that. She laughed, appreciating the humour that was part of Titus' character. Another text message popped up. This time it was Thomas, just saying good night and that he loved her. Her finger traced the hearts that had accompanied the message.

Heading for bed, Thomas hesitated for a moment. He had a thought about why they were going through what they were. He reached for the pad of paper and pen that he kept beside his bed and jotted it down. He then bent his head in prayer, waiting for God's peace to come. At last, he drew the covers over himself and slept, seeking refreshment from that.

Chapter 36

Standing behind the pharmacy counter on the Wednesday following that, Taran watched her customers closely. She still felt uneasy being there, afraid of the customers and worried for her staff. She just didn't know when the next attack would come and who would be hurt when that happened.

Joe's eyes kept watching Taran and then the store as well. He could feel the tension and worry in Taran and didn't know what to say to relieve that. He simply went about his daily tasks, keeping an eye on her as he could. They worked together well as a team. Joe was grateful for that. The last few months with George had been tense.

Taran turned at the end of the day, thanking her staff. She stopped beside Joe, sensing that he wanted to talk to her.

"Joe? What are your thoughts?"

"About what? What you and Thomas are going through?" Joe had thought it through.

"About that? We think it goes back to our fathers and grandfathers." Taran didn't want to say too much and hurt Aidan's investigation.

Joe stared at her for a moment before he nodded.

"I agree with that assessment, Taran. It never made sense for it to be just about you and Thomas. I can see that. And I have a good idea who." Joe said a name, Taran's eyes closing as he did so.

"Joe? We need you to talk with the guys. Can you do that?" Taran was desperate to have this over with. She just wanted to get on with her life.

"I can do that. When?" Joe had his Bible study and prayer group that night but would gladly set it aside for Taran.

"Tonight? We're meeting at my place for a meal and then for a time of prayer. We plan on working on this as well. Could you make it? Eva is welcome to join us as well." Eva was Joe's wife and a friend of Taran's.

"We can do that. She's been wanting to help but just didn't know how to." Joe walked away, waiting for Taran to lock up before he walked her to her car. "We'll be there shortly. Eva will bring something for the meal." He waved as Taran drove off.

Aidan stopped in Taran's kitchen, seeing the number of people who had gathered. He had not expected that. However, everyone he needed to speak with was gathered there.

"Aidan? Have you eaten?" Rachel approached him.

"No, I haven't." He took the plate of food handed to him before he found somewhere to sit. "Thank you, Rachel. This smells so good."

Their meal finished and their time of prayer over, the group gathered in the living room, the largest room in the house. The men found places on the floor, allowing the ladies the seats. Thomas sat at Taran's feet, an elbow resting on her knee. Her hand was on it while her eyes were on Aidan.

"Aidan? What can you tell us?" Thomas spoke at last, his eyes on his father.

"Okay. There is some news that I can tell you. The man who abducted you the last time, Taran? Unfortunately, he has never spoken. He died last night from a heart attack. The emergency personnel was unable to revive him." He gave a small smile at the look on her face.

"So, we don't know who hired him." Taran was frustrated.

"Not confirmed. But with what you have done and what Emma has sent us, we're closing in on the man and who he is associated with. You were correct in your suspicion that it goes back for decades. There is a lot of work proving that, though."

"There would be." Tam spoke at last, his words causing Aidan to reach quickly for his notepad and pen.

Jotting down his notes, Aidan paused. This was the information that he was missing, he decided. He excused himself, walking away and back to the office. He was not to be there but this investigation was driving him to do that. Toryn shook his head as he walked across the parking lot to his car and saw Aidan's vehicle back in the lot. He would need to talk with him tomorrow about taking time off.

The group watched Aidan walk away before they looked at one another. This was where it became more dangerous for the couple and they wanted to avoid any more trouble coming to him. They just didn't know how to.

Thomas reached for the paperwork that he had dropped on the floor beside him. Taran leaned forward, an elbow on his shoulder, to read with him. Her finger pointed to a name.

"That name? He's prominent in Elmton. Who do we talk to there?" Taran looked up as she heard another voice.

Richard walked in on the group, having felt compelled to reach out to them. Don nodded at him even as he handed over his sheaf of papers.

"Richard. You're here. We need your input on this name." Don pointed it out.

Richard studied the paper, knowing that they had put the name to someone who had been in the eyesight of local authorities. His name had not been known but his criminal activities had been. His phone was out as he called a friend on the force.

"Bill?" Richard had reached out to Bill Buckley, the lead detective on the force. "That man who we've been trying to identify for years? Here's his name. It came up in the investigation into what Thomas and Taran are going through." He listened for a few moments before he pocketed his phone. He knew that Bill would find the evidence that was needed and make the arrest. Bill had indicated that they only needed a name to finish it off and Richard had supplied that.

Taran waited for Richard to speak, watching as he assembled his thoughts. He looked up directly at her and nodded. She drew in a sigh of relief. At least one of the men would disappear from their adventure. They now had to find the information that would help find the others.

Thomas reached for her hand, finding it cold. He rubbed at it, his thoughts muddled for a moment. He knew that their danger was not over, not by a long shot as Titus would have said. They had to live life whether or not they were still in danger. That worried him.

Don watched the group in the living room, nodding to himself. Joe had provided information that they had been missing, coming from a different perspective than they had. Eva had been able to help as well, giving information on the families that they didn't have.

Chapter 37

Saturday found Taran in the pharmacy, working for a change on the weekend. She had traded with Joe for a day off earlier in the week. She needed to find another pharmacist if business kept picking up. That puzzled her, that the business was growing as it was when it hadn't under George. Taran couldn't understand that.

Looking up as she felt a presence near her, her face lit up. Thomas had dropped her off at work that morning, a kiss on her cheek to warm her through the day. He had now appeared in front of her.

"Almost done, my darlin'?"

"I am. Just a few more tasks." Taran moved quickly with the pharmacy technician to set away the tools of their trade and lock up what needed to be done. She accepted the locked money bag from the sales staff and headed for her office, locking it into her safe. She reached for her purse, pausing for a moment to thank God for a safe day and asking that it continued.

Thomas tucked Taran into his truck, his hand resting on the door for a moment as he searched the area. He felt safe that night, not feeling anyone watching him. That did bother him as there should have been. Their adventure was not over, not yet.

Taran watched Thomas and then searched the area herself. She felt someone out there but didn't worry. Thomas was with her. She trusted his instincts in keeping her safe. Taran shifted on her seat as

Thomas slid behind the wheel of his truck and then just sat.

"Thomas? What are you thinking?" Taran wasn't sure what to think at that moment. Thomas was silent and that was unusual for him.

"Taran, I love you. I don't want to wait for months for you to be my life mate and helpmeet. Will you marry me?" Thomas shifted himself on his seat, to turn to face her. He reached for her hands, his grasp strong and warm on hers.

Taran stared at him, remembering at last to close her mouth. She has thought this was coming but had not expected it so soon. She realized that they did know one another better than most couples did when they were at this stage.

Blinking back tears, she nodded, unable to speak. He simply reached to hug her, a kiss on her lips. She sat back, staring at him for a moment.

"I love you, too, Thomas. I don't want to wait either. So, how do we do this?" She grinned as he grinned and shook his head.

"We make plans, my darlin'. And then we go forward with them. Come on. We need to celebrate. He drove away, happiness radiating in the cab of the truck. Neither of them saw the vehicle that had approached and then followed them.

Taran walked through her home that night, a glow on her face. Thomas had placed a beautiful ruby ring on her finger. She was floating, she knew but also had to face the reality that this was not over for them.

———

Thomas strode through his yard, intent on finding what was showing up on his security feed. Something was back there and he was determined to solve that mystery that night. His feet slowed as he approached the lump lying there. Backing away, he pulled out his phone. That was a body there and he had no intention of getting any closer.

Aidan approached Thomas an hour later. The teams were still working around the area. The coroner had been on site and the body had been examined and then loaded into a body bag before being removed. He knew that Thomas wasn't responsible. He had an approximate time of death for the man and knew that Thomas had been with Taran at a restaurant. He had observed them there himself.

"Thomas? I know you didn't do this. I saw you and Taran in the restaurant. This has been left as a threat directed at you. You know that they mean to kill you, don't you?" Aidan's voice and face were stern as he asked that question.

Thomas shrugged. It was about what he had expected to hear.

"I gathered that. I didn't see you tonight." He grinned as Aidan laughed. "I guess Taran and me were wrapped up in our conversation."

"I would say that you were. Anything that you want to tell me?" Aidan laughed again as Thomas shook his head.

"But what about that man? Do we know who he is?" Thomas' thoughts turned to that.

"We do. I'm not releasing it yet until we notify the next of kin. But I can assure you that he is involved in this in a way that I wish he wasn't."

Thomas nodded, hearing what Aidan was not saying to him. That was about what he figured. He had trouble sleeping that night, the scene cleared shortly before midnight. His thoughts drifted to his lady and a smile crossed his face. He slept, not realizing that Sunday would start off the worse week of their lives, with danger creeping closer and closer to them until it would culminate in a horrible way.

Taran rose the next morning, a song on her lips. It was Sunday and they were heading for church together. This would be the first Sunday there as an official couple. Thomas had agreed that they would not rush their wedding but he didn't want to wait. They would try and speak with Gideon, their minister, that day. They had arranged a meal at Thomas' parents' home with Taran's parents present. Neither one of them doubted that their engagement would be much of a surprise.

Tam turned as his daughter approached him, reaching to hug her. His hand went out to shake Thomas'. Instead, he wrapped him in a hug. He sensed that the couple had reached a decision, and if it was what he and Rachel suspected, it would come as no surprise to any one of them.

Thomas stood at the end of the meal, his hands resting on Taran's shoulders. He waited for quiet before he began to speak. His words reassured the families that they were taking as many precautions as they could to stay safe. None of the ones present felt easy about the week. They all sensed that something was coming and that meant danger to the couple in front of them.

His eyes dropped to the top of Taran's head. His hands tightened on her shoulders before he raised his eyes, searching each one present. They had had a chance to speak with Gideon that morning, and a wedding date had been set for two weeks from then. They had assured one another that they could and would be ready for it.

Not surprised at the news, the families rose to hug and congratulate the couple. Rachel held on to her daughter a little tighter, knowing that she was setting sail on a new sea of life, one that would take her from her family and into Thomas' life. That was only right and proper. Her prayer rose for them, knowing that they were still not safe.

Tam and Thaddeus approached Thomas and Titus later as the two younger men sat on the back deck. Rose and Rachel had drawn Taran into the office to help her with her plans. Taran had a deer-in-the-headlights look for a moment before she had smiled a huge smile. This was what she needed. God had provided the mothers that were just right for them both.

"Son? Where does the investigation stand?" Thaddeus sat down near his son.

"Not where we want it to be. I found a body in the backyard last night. Aidan knows who it is but he's not saying."

The two older men stared at him for a moment.

"You did say a body?" Tam confirmed that. "A threat towards you?"

"That's what we think. I am afraid for Taran. I think this week will be the culmination, Dad. I don't know that we're prepared for this but we have to be. Please, please, pray for us. God is the only one who can defend us." Thomas' head went down as he tried to draw in strength from within.

Chapter 38

Thomas walked towards the office building the next morning, a spring in his steps. He was happy but still troubled, if that combination was at all possible. He headed for his office, dropping the files that he was carrying on the desk. With a mug of coffee in hand, Thomas headed back for his office. None of the others were there yet but that didn't surprise him. He was earlier than he normally was.

A sound about thirty minutes later had Thomas raising his head. He frowned at the stumbling steps that he heard and was on his feet. In the hallway, Thomas came to an abrupt halt, his hands rising in the air. Joshua stood there, blood trickling down from a cut above his eyebrow. His eyes were clouded. Thomas stared at him and then at the men behind him. He recognized the one. He had been seen around Taran's pharmacy in the last few days. This was not how he planned to start his Monday nor was it how he had wanted Joshua to start his.

Motioned forward, Thomas stood for a moment with his hands in the air. When the weapon in the man's hand was turned and dug into Joshua's temple, Thomas's feet took him slowly forward. He was shoved forward and out of the door, Joshua's steps sounding behind him. They were forced into a vehicle and the vehicle sped away, leaving a cloud of dust that settled down without leaving any evidence of what had happened.

Don frowned as he entered the building. The trucks that were in the parking lot belonged to Thomas and Joshua. Only neither man was in the building. He searched each office and then outside. Mark, Paul, and Caleb walked towards him, exchanging glances as they did so. It didn't look like good news, they each decided, not with the look on Don's face.

"Don?" Mark spoke for the trio.

"We have a problem. Thomas and Joshua are missing. Their trucks are here. They're not." Don rubbed at the back of his neck. This is not what he wanted to tell the others.

Mark was past him and into the office, heading for the security room and then pulling up the video feed. He paused as he saw Joshua taken down and then shoved towards the building and then a few minutes later the two men were forced out and into a vehicle. He was on his feet and back out of the office, heading towards where Don had walked to.

"Both Joshua and Thomas have been taken. I have a good picture that I can print off. We'll need to call in Aidan."

"Already done." Don held up his phone. "We need to stand back and let them work." Don pointed to his house. "In there, fellows. Mark, you can pull up the feed from there. We'll look at it and see what we can determine."

Caleb pulled out his phone, answering a call before he waved and walked away. Taran had called, worried that Thomas had not called her when he said he would. She was at work and he headed that way.

He found Taran watching for one of them. She waved and pointed towards her office.

When she was able to, Taran took her break and headed for Caleb, fear for Thomas rising in her heart. If Thomas had been okay, she knew, she would have heard from him.

"Caleb? When?" Taran stopped just inside the door, her arms wrapping around her abdomen to stop them from shaking.

"I'm sorry, Taran. Joshua and Thomas were abducted from the building. Thomas seems okay. Joshua was taken down. We're not sure how badly he was hurt." Caleb watched her closely, reading to make her sit if necessary.

"I see. They've increased their actions against us, haven't they? I need to work today. Titus made sure that I got to work. Thomas was to pick me up." Taran chewed at her bottom lip, trying to decide who to call to pick her up.

"One of us will be here when you close, Taran. It's what we do. You are part of our family and we take care of our family." Caleb takes a moment to pray with her before he walked away.

Taran stood for a few moments, lost in thought, before she returned to her work. It would be a long day, she thought.

Caleb walked back into the store at closing time, ready to take Taran to where they were hoping to keep her safe. There were no guarantees on that, they all knew. The men had proven that they would go after either one of the couple wherever they could.

Taran paced Don's home, knowing that she was where she needed to be. She just wasn't happy about it. She sighed and found a corner to hide in, her head bowed as she sought for answers from God. Taran knew that she just might not like the answers that came.

Aidan found her at last, a few hours after she had arrived. He sat quietly near her, waiting for Taran to look up. She did at last, her eyes focusing on him at last.

"Aidan, have you found them?"

Aidan shook his head. He wished that he had but they were just not found. He didn't know where they were.

"I'm sorry, Taran. We haven't. We have photos of the men who took them which gives us their names. We just don't know where they're hiding. We need to keep you safe or they'll take you hostage as well."

Taran frowned at his choice of words. She had not thought of it that way.

"Taken as a hostage? That's an interesting choice of words."

"That's what it is, Taran. We know enough that is what the purpose of all this is. They want to take both of you hostage again to get back at your fathers. We have a good idea why but we need some more proof about that." He looked around as Tam and Thaddeus entered and sat close to them. "Tam?

Thaddeus? We know pretty much why this has happened. Our task right now is to keep Taran safe. They'll take her to use her against you two just as they have taken Thomas. Joshua was not meant to be taken, we don't think. He just happened to be there."

"Solve this and soon, Aidan. If you don't, then we go looking. And the consequences of that won't be what they should be." Thaddeus was deeply worried about his son. It was coming to a head, he knew, and that worried him more than he could utter.

Chapter 39

Thomas paced the office that he and Joshua were locked into. He turned to Joshua, finding him slumped in a chair, his head in his hands. He must have a horrible headache, Thomas decided, searching for anything that would help relieve it. He didn't find anything.

Turning back to the door, Thomas tugged at it again, finding it still locked. He didn't like this. They had had no chance to defend themselves that morning. That disturbed him greatly. Whoever it was after him was watching him very closely, he could tell. He prayed for safety for his lady and his team. His thoughts to his father and Taran's father. He prayed for safety for them as well.

Joshua looked up, his eyes clearer than they had been. His head was pounding, he had to admit. The men had been on him far too quickly for him to react that morning.

"Thomas? Did you recognize any of them?" Joshua was praying that he had.

"No. I wish that I did. Did you?"

"No, it happened far too quickly. I was down and then hauled to my feet in a matter of seconds after I left my truck." Joshua rose, wavered on his feet for a moment, and then too began to pace the room. "Where are we?"

"In an office building downtown. We are on the first floor but the windows? We would need to break them and I don't want to take a chance on that. Not yet anyway." Thomas was frustrated. He wanted out of there and he wanted vengeance. Only vengeance wasn't his to dole out. That was God's.

"I wonder if anyone saw us being brought in." Joshua stopped at a window, staring out. He jumped back in surprise, a low yell alerting Thomas that something was wrong.

Thomas was beside him, his eyes on the youth standing at the window. He recognized him as one that Ben helped. The youth waved and then disappeared. A few moments later, they heard the sound of a lock being turned and the door opening towards them. They followed the youth, their footsteps as quiet as they could make them. Running from the building, the two men followed the youth as he headed away from the building and deeper into the downtown area.

Ducking into a building, Thomas leaned against a wall, a hand out to steady Joshua for a moment. They both listened for anyone following them before they were on the move again, this time heading away from the downtown area. They made their way as rapidly as they could towards the police department.

The desk officer looked up in surprise as he saw them before he motioned them through to head towards Aidan's office, visitor badges handed to them. Aidan looked up in surprise as the men appeared, shutting the door behind them before he was away and back with coffee and muffins for them.

"Here. Eat these. We'll talk." Aidan was back in his chair, working through what he had on his desk.

He waited for a few moments before he looked up to find both men staring at him. He sat back, questioning how they arrived there.

"Aidan? Taran? Is she okay?" Thomas' first thought was for his lady;

"She is. Caleb took her to Don's and won't let her leave there until she's due at work tomorrow. She'll be safe there. Talk to me, guys. Tell me what happened."

"I arrived at work and was working away when I heard a sound. I found Joshua in the hallway with a gun on him. They took us to the Bell building downtown and locked us in. A youth from the street freed us." Thomas shared a look with Aidan. There was no way that he was giving a name.

Aidan nodded. He wouldn't push the men to tell him. He knew that they wouldn't give a name. That was fair, he decided. He would put out word on the street with a reward for the youth. He could claim it at Ben's.

Joshua then told him what had happened to him. He could give few details of the men, not having had a clear look at them. Aidan nodded at him as well before he was on his feet.

"Let's get you to Don's. We'll stop at your places for you to grab some clean clothes and then you're staying with Don until this is over. Joshua, you are at risk right now just because of today."

Taran jumped as she felt arms around her, arms that were familiar and belonged to a man who loved her and who she loved. She struggled in them in order to turn and wrap her arms around Thomas. She didn't care how he got there. She was glad that he was.

"Thomas? What happened?" Taran leaned against him, content to be held and to have him with her.

"I had an adventure without you. Joshua went with me. We're free, my darlin'. We need to solve this and now."

"Who?" Taran leaned back to look up at him.

"Whoever owns the Bell building. That's where we were held. We need to do some research, my love, but for now, I need to clean up and then we eat. Daci has a meal ready for us, she says." Thomas moved reluctantly away from Taran, not wanting to let her go.

Taran watched him walk away before she turned to Don.

"Don, how do we do this? How do we find the ones responsible?"

"We know who they are. Emma just sent word. We need to keep you and Thomas here for now with my team. Richard and his team are heading this way tomorrow to help. Aidan has the names that he needs. It's the dangerous part of the adventure for you. With Thomas getting away as he did, they'll be looking for either you or him. If they get their hands on you, you will not survive. We can guarantee that. Now, we'll eat. Then, we'll spend some time in prayer. We plan on working through the night to finalize what we have.

Aidan has asked us to keep you here. Your families are tucked away under police protection.'

Thomas watched Taran closely over the next few hours, rising at last just to gather her into his arms and then tuck her into her bed. She was asleep before he pulled the covers over her. He stood and watched her for a few moments before he dropped a kiss on her temple and then walked away.

Feeling anger growing in him, Thomas had to pray to have it removed. He knew that it was a natural feeling to have but he wanted to let God have the glory in this. It was how he felt as a Christian. Now, they just had to do what they could to find the man responsible.

Aidan had been around. He told the men that they were arresting the men's employees from the bottom of the line upwards. They were closer to him but he had gone into hiding. They just didn't know where. He warned Thomas that they needed to be very careful at this point. Thomas had simply nodded at that, knowing it was true.

Chapter 40

Two days later, Thomas stood in the shadow of a building near the Bell building. They had received word that Edwin Bell had returned and was in the building. Thomas watched as police officers moved to surround the building. He observed Aidan heading inside and prayed for his friend and the other officers involved. There was no guarantee that Bell would give himself up without shooting first. And if he did that, shots would be returned and he more than likely would not survive. It would be justice if he didn't but they might not get the answers that they were looking for if that happened.

His team stood shoulder to shoulder with him, their eyes on the building as well. Aidan had reached out to let them know that they were raiding the building. He was aware that the team would show up but would stay out of the way unless they were needed.

Hours passed before Aidan reappeared, a disheveled look to his clothing. Thomas frowned at that. He didn't like that. Aidan stood for a moment, his face turned up to the sun as his eyes closed. It was over for Thomas and Taran. It had not ended as they wanted it to but it had ended as God willed. And it was His will that mattered.

Walking towards Thomas and his team, Aidan felt the fatigue that was weighing him down. It always did when a case closed.

"Aidan?" Don spoke for the group, his eyes on Thomas.

"It's over, Thomas. It's finally over. Give me a couple of days and I'll meet with you and Taran and your families. Your team as well." Aidan hesitated, knowing that he had to speak.

"He put up a fight." Thomas' question was not a question but a statement.

"He did. Unfortunately, he did. He pulled a weapon on us and refused to put it down. He shot at one of the officers. When they returned fire, he was hit and killed. We'll be a while processing this building and his home." Aidan walked away, feeling the prayers of his friends in his heart.

Thomas slumped back against the wall, his eyes closing. *Thank you, Lord. It's over for my lady. Aidan will talk with us, but You brought us through this. We would not have survived without Your protection and defense of us.*

Thomas felt a hand on his arm and turned. Don stood beside him, his eyes closed as he prayed for his friend. The others followed, bringing Thomas to the throne of God. They walked away after a while, relief in their minds and hearts but questions still remained.

Taran turned from looking out of the office window as she heard footsteps. Thomas had appeared and then just opened his arms. Taran launched herself at him, his arms folding her close to his heart. They just stood for a while, neither one speaking and neither one moving.

Taran leaned back at last, her eyes on Thomas. She could see that something had happened, something that lightened his heart.

———

213

"Thomas?"

"It's over, my darlin'. It's over. All but Aidan giving us the reasons why. Edwin Bell decided to get into a fight with the police. He didn't survive. He refused to come out when asked to." Thomas tightened his arms around her, feeling her sobs as she broke down. All he could do was pray for healing for his lady and for himself.

Don had approached and then walked away. They needed this time together, he knew. Daci was watching him and then hugged her brother. They turned to walk towards the outdoors, knowing that they were free once more to do that.

"Don? What happened?" Daci had not asked when the men first returned.

"Edwin Bell? He's dead. He fought the police and it didn't go his way." Don was tired and relieved but still worried. Something was off, he decided, that involved him. He just didn't know what.

Walking through her home that night, Taran felt tired but relieved. She knew that Thomas was at home and safe. Her family was safe as was his. Now, all they needed to do was find out the reason why.

She stopped in her office, her eyes on the plans for her wedding the next week. She was relieved that they were not in danger any more and that they could move freely through that day without watching out for someone coming after them. Her face was softened as she thought of Thomas. He was truly the knight that she had dreamed about. God had protected him that day and she was so thankful for that.

Thomas sought out his favourite seat on the back deck, his inevitable cup of coffee in his hand. He was exhausted, the mental and emotional strain of the past weeks that had drawn his strength gone. He was happy about that. His own thoughts turned to Taran. He thanked God that their adventure was over, even though they still didn't know the true reason why. That would come in a few days.

Don too found a seat on his back deck, the only lights on coming from the solar lights. He was thankful as well that Thomas and Taran were safe. He just wanted to know why. His thoughts turned to prayer as he prayed for the couple and their families. His prayers turned to his sister and then his team. They were not through with their adventures, he didn't think, and time would prove him right.

Chapter 41

Walking into Thomas' house two days later, Aidan smiled as he heard the happy voices and laughter that permeated the atmosphere. He was relieved for Thomas and Taran and their families. He had news for them, news that he had not expected to find. He wondered when he was told how much that Thaddeus and Tam knew of the reason why. Aidan had not been expecting what he heard.

Taran turned as she felt an arm across her shoulders and hugged Aidan. She had come to think of him as a friend and not just an investigator. Thomas was a close friend of his and she knew that it pleased him that Taran now counted Aidan as a friend.

Their meal finished and their time of prayer completed, all eyes turned towards Aidan. Toryn had appeared as they ate, gladly accepting a meal. He studied each one who was present, his eyes lingering the longest on Thomas and Taran.

Thaddeus shared a look with Rose and then with Tam and Rachel before he looked over at Thomas. Thomas sat on the floor at Taran's feet, her hand on his shoulder. They looked happy, he thought, and prayed that Aidan would have answers for them.

"Thomas. Taran." Aidan's voice cut through the silence that had settled in the room, a good silence he decided. "I can't say how sorry I am that we couldn't solve this before this all transpired. It just wasn't to be. We all know that God is in control and everything that happens is in His timing.

"Now, as it regards Edwin Bell? You were correct when you stated that it all went back to your grandfathers. Tam and Thaddeus? I don't know how much you are aware of the rivalry that was there."

Tam shook his head, seeing Thaddeus do the same.

"I had no idea of any rivalry. I know that Dad avoided Bell's father and that he didn't like him." Tam responded, not sure where Aidan was going with his words.

"The same of my Dad. He didn't like Bell senior and made sure that we avoided him at all costs." Thaddeus reached for Rose's hand and held on to it. There had always been a current in the family that was not solved.

"That's what we've been told. I can't tell you the number of people who have come forward in the last two days now that Bell is dead. He was a vicious, cruel, spiteful man. What Thomas and Taran went through? It was directed at you two. I'll explain that in a moment. For now, I need to do a bit of background that you might now be aware of.

"Bell senior was involved in crime since his youth. He wanted to expand his territory and your fathers refused to sell their property to him. He tried everything he could short of arson and murder to get them to do that. When he died, his son picked up on that and tried it with your fathers and then with you two. He didn't want your businesses. He wanted the property that you own outside of town. He planned to set up a drug manufacturing place. Bell planned to take over your pharmacy, Taran, and was blackmailing George. George had done some things that almost crossed the line into criminality that Bell was aware of. Apparently, he had threatened to go to the pharmacy college and report him, hoping that he would lose the pharmacy. He wanted it to bring in his supplies through a legitimate company. When you bought George out, he saw an opportunity to bring harm to you and hurt your father as well. He hadn't planned on Thomas being there. How do we know this? He kept detailed notes, which will help prosecute his underlings."

"He kept notes?" Thomas was surprised at that and then nodded. Of course, he would. Isn't that what they did?

Taran studied Aidan as he spoke and then looked at her father.

"Dad? Did you know this?"

Tam shook his head, his eyes on his daughter.

"Not at all, Taran. Not at all. We would have taken steps to stop him if we had known. No one had much to do with him all his life. This is likely why. I feel sorry for him. He never had the chance that we had, being raised by parents who cared for us and looked out for all areas of our lives. It shows how much we need God in our lives."

"That we do. I would have to echo Tam's words. We never had contact with him outside of class. Anyone who had anything to do with him was avoided as well. They were always the ones in trouble." Thaddeus echoed Tam's words.

"He didn't have any family, did he?" Taran's thoughts had moved on from what Aidan said.

"No, he didn't. That was something else he had against your fathers, Taran and Thomas. No lady wanted anything to do with them."

"That's so sad. A life ruined because of his father. I'm so glad that God gave us the families that we have." Taran's hand tightened on Thomas' shoulder and his hand reached to grasp hers.

"God provides for us in all things. And that includes our families."

They talked for a while longer before they left. Taran was the last to leave, spending some time with her sweetheart. They prayed together before Thomas hugged her and walked her to her car. He watched as she drove away, confident that she would make it home safely this time.

That Saturday, Thomas paced in Gideon's office. He was nervous yet happy, if there could be such a combination. Today was the day that he married his sweetheart and darling, Taran. They had been through enough to draw them close as friends and as a couple.

Taran was confident in Thomas' love. She was dressed in her mother's wedding dress that had been kept carefully for her if she wanted it. She had always dreamed of wearing it to meet her knight at the front of a church. Today was that day. Taran turned as her father touched her arm before he hugged her.

Tam stood and studied his daughter, his hands holding hers. He nodded. Thomas was her soulmate, that much he knew. They had spent hours speaking. Knowing Thaddeus through the years but not his son had helped. He knew how Thomas had been raised in the Christian faith.

Turning later that afternoon, Thomas looked for Taran, finding her standing with Daci and Payten. The female members of Richard's team were there as well as the wives of the male members. Richard and the husbands and his team members were around, mingling with their friends and families.

Titus stood by his brother, not saying a word. It wasn't necessary.

"Thomas? How are you?" Titus broke the silence at last.

"I'm okay, Titus. We're working through what happened, as a team, with Taran, and by myself. We're getting there." He smiled as Taran looked up and found his gaze on her.

Taran excused herself, moving among the friends and families, accepting hugs and kisses as they were given to her. She found herself wrapped in Thomas' arms and kissed. She was content, feeling safe and cherished and loved. They both knew that there would be difficulties in their lives, but with God defending them and providing for them, they had no doubt that they would make it through, walking hand in hand with one another.

Toryn and Aidan approached them, smiles on their faces. Both men were slightly envious of Thomas, wanting that helpmeet and lady in their own lives. They were content to wait for God's timing but they both prayed that they didn't have to go through what both Paul and Thomas had faced.

Don watched his paramedic, the one who he depended on for medical issues. Thomas had spoken at length with him about what had happened to him. They had not been able to fully explain what had happened to Thomas and Taran.

The families gathered around the couple, the fathers praying for them and giving them their blessings. They had grown closer over the past weeks, ending that they had many interests in common.

Walking out to Thomas' truck early that evening, Taran still looked for someone coming after them. She felt eyes on her that day but this time, the eyes were not those of people bringing danger to them. They were instead the eyes of friends.

Thomas reached to kiss her, hugging her to him. They were starting a new chapter of their book of life. He was glad that it was Taran with him. She was indeed his soulmate and the lady that he had been waiting for.

"Happy, my darlin'?" Thomas drove off, his hand reaching for Taran's.

"I am, Thomas. If we had not gone through what we had, I don't know that we would have met. God protected us and brought us together. Thank you for being who you are."

Silence filled the cab of the truck as Thomas drove away from the church. They were off to a little cabin in the woods for the next week before they were back to work. God had been with them all the steps that they had taken. He had not left them nor forsaken them.

———

Thank you for choosing to read the story of Thomas and Taran. As always, they have taken the story on the path that they have chosen. As the writer, I am just along for the ride, putting down their words.

Through it all, they were firm in their belief that God was there with them, that He both protected and defended them. He also kept His promise never to leave them or forsake them. That is something that we have confidence in. God is there every step of our daily walk. We may turn and walk away from Him at times, but He never does that to us.

And as usual, other characters have shown up in the story. Richard and his team have their stories in *His Protectors*. Abe and Emma and his team have their stories in *His Guardians*. Samuel and Aideen and their friends have their stories in *His Warriors*. For some reason, my characters always walk through other stories. I enjoy bringing the characters together. I miss the ones whose stories I have finished.

God bless each one of you as you travel this journey through life. Keep your eyes on God.

Ronna

Website: ronnabacon.com